ANNIE'S STORY

*A Novel of
Psychological Suspense*

by

Peter Gilboy

Praise for Peter Gilboy's

Madeleine's Kiss

"Uniquely Gripping"

"Riveting and eye-opening"

"Defies the common label of 'thriller' or 'mystery.'"

"The reviewer loves a surprise. And nothing has surprised more than the revelations in *Madeleine's Kiss*."

—Midwest Book Reviews

First published by Dog Ear Publishing
4011 Vincennes Rd
Indianapolis, IN 46268
www.dogearpublishing.net

ISBN: 978-1-4575-3985-5

This book is printed on acid-free paper.

This book is a work of fiction. Places, events, and situations in this book
are purely Fictional and any resemblance to actual persons, living or dead,
is coincidental.

Printed in the United States of America

Thank you!

Once again, many thanks to my first readers—William Hawkes, Bonnie Nicholson and Preston Dane for your suggestions, corrections, admonitions and excitement over the *Annie's Story*.

And, as always, thank you to Jane Claire Collins who made everything possible.

One final thank you.
To Crazy Quilt Entertainment
for its support of *Annie's Story*.

Peter Gilboy can be reached at
Hello@PeterGilboy.com
Or though his website at
www.PeterGilboy.com

This story is dedicated to
Jack McClurg

PART I

1

**Men are more moral than they think
and far more immoral than they can imagine.
-Sigmund Freud**

I'M NINETEEN NOW AND NO LONGER A GIRL. I'm a woman in every way that counts. It's not just because of my age but because of my experiences too. I don't mean sexual experiences. I know things I didn't know before. I know about violence and betrayal. And I know the darkest lie of all.

My dad, the well-known shrink, says it's okay to remember everything but that I need to somehow verbalize my anger in the right ways. He says it can be cathartic, which means cleansing or an emotional release. He doesn't want what's inside me to accumulate into rage. Always the therapist, Dad would like me to join some group where we sit around in a circle and swap stories about how bad things happen to good people — *Oh, I'm so sorry, Annie . . .That's so awful!* . . . or, *Annie, how did that make you feel?*

No talk therapy for me. I don't need sympathy and I don't want my words to escape into thin air. I need to understand. So I'm going to say it all right here, just put it down on the page so I can go over it again and again, and so others will understand what I have to do now. Maybe my anger and sadness will all slip away then. Maybe I'll be okay.

Maybe I really will.

Everything happened in Windham, so I guess I should start there. Windham is a neat and tidy town in Upstate New York. Some people would say it's *quaint* and others would call it *socially remote*. No great artists lived in Windham and no great events ever occurred there except for sudden storms in the summer or winter that could either flood the town or bury it in snow. Trailways goes through Windham, but not often. There were no murders in anyone's memory, no rapes or molestations or sudden disappearances. It's a quiet town. Windham was perfect, we thought. Safe and sound, and that's where Veronica and I would grow up.

We moved there ten years ago. That was in April 2005. I was nine and my little sister Veronica was almost three. My dad, Dr. Simon Taylor, had made a bunch from the popularity of his book, and it was number four on the best-seller list and still holding fast. I'll bet fifty thousand a month was tumbling in, and Dad had already signed a two million dollar advance on his next book. That's a lot of money for a Freudian therapist turned self-help writer. So we got out of the City.

When we moved to Windham, I didn't have to worry about going to malls or McDonald's or having cool hideaways to go to with my soon-to-be boyfriends. There aren't any places like that. Just a pizza shop, a real estate office, a funeral home next to a Methodist church, a winery, a ski shop, and a gas station with a country store — Mitch's, where retired men bring their own coffee cups and sit at wooden tables and make conversation.

Our house on Mill Street was from the 1920's, and had been built by one of the earlier town leaders. It was bigger than almost any of the other houses — two stories with a high-peaked roof and perfect fish-scale trim above the small attic windows that I could climb up to and look out of. It also had a wraparound porch that Mom used to sit on, put her feet up on the railing and cross her ankles. We also had a wooden swing in the front yard, and like everyone else on our street we had a manicured lawn. The only thing we didn't have was a white picket fence. My mom, Sunny Taylor, said she loved our new white house but she would miss the excitement of the City, by which she meant the break-ins and shootings. So Windham it was.

We had a dog, too, Rainbow, who had one leg missing. He was a five-year-old Australian Shepard that Mom had found at the shelter. He was all black, thus the name Rainbow. My mom's idea. Dad wondered if Rainbow could really get along with only one front paw, but Mom told him Rainbow was left-handed, so he'd be fine. Turns out that he's also a creek dog. When he wasn't chasing birds he'd be wading in the creek behind our house and gulping up minnows.

When we moved to Windham we were the outsiders. Neighbors waved and smiled politely, but we were from the City and probably liberals, so we weren't to be trusted. We didn't have a truck with four-wheel drive and we didn't hunt in the state forest or fish over at North Lake. Mom drove a Honda minivan and Dad had a new, red Saab convertible. I'm sure everyone suspected we didn't own a gun at all. Even the fact that Dad was a best-selling author didn't help. People smiled and called him *Dr. Taylor* when they ran into him at the store, but at school I remember my new fourth grade teacher Miss Witherspoon telling a parent that his best-selling book was *smutty and obscene*. I didn't know what that meant, and had to ask my dad. He said that it meant *offensive*, but I wasn't sure what that meant either. Dad added that some people wouldn't understand how important his book was, but that I would when I got older.

Mom agreed that Dad's book wasn't smutty or obscene. If it was the truth, she said, then that's the only thing that mattered. Mom was from India. She was a Sikh, and she always said— "Annie, truth is something lofty, and worth pursing at any cost. Never be afraid of the truth."

She didn't say that truth is also a knife that can open your veins.

2

**In matters of sexuality we are at present—
every one of us—nothing but hypocrites.
-Sigmund Freud**

IN SMALL TOWNS LIKE WINDHAM there aren't any local police or detectives, only the state police or what we called the Staties. When you dial 911, it's the Staties who answer the phone and who come to help. That's what my dad did on October 24, 2005. He called 911. He knew it was a TV myth that the police had to wait twenty-four hours. But he was still afraid they might not take him all that seriously. They had seen it all before—the husband finally makes it home from work to the impatient wife; the wife limps in with a bruised ankle after being caught up in shopping spree somewhere; or the drunk sobers up and returns home shamefaced. But the state troopers came right away, within twenty minutes, even though my mom had only been gone for an hour.

I remember three of them in two cars, a dark grey cruiser with a light rack on top and another cruiser trying to look like a regular car. I also remember the tall African-American trooper with perfect posture, black-rimmed glasses, and a hat that was almost like Smokey the Bear's. His name was Trooper Reginald Wood, and he was clearly the one in charge. He's retired now, but when he took the stand at my dad's trial I remembered how serious his face was when he came to our house that day.

Trooper Wood didn't take the situation lightly. He asked my dad some quick questions, and then, with the other two officers, he immediately searched the house top to bottom. But they could find no sign of a broken window, a forced door, no evidence of a kidnapping at all, and no body had been reported anywhere, no suicide off the nearest bridge. Trooper Wood asked if any of my mom's clothes were missing, as if she might have packed suddenly and walked away to a new life with someone else, maybe even take on a new identity. It's common enough. The records show that he also checked the sex offender database to see what dangerous people might be living nearby. No one in Windham. No one within twenty-five miles.

Trooper Wood asked all the right questions about my mom, Sunny Taylor, and took lots of notes including what prescription medication she might have been on. *None.* Any psychiatric issues? *No.* Was she despondent or depressed or angry that morning? *No.* Forgetful? *Never.* Had she ever had a stroke? *No.* What about arguments? Had there been any? *No.* Trooper Wood asked another question then: *Could there . . . be someone else?* Dad looked at him. He knew what he meant and couldn't help but laugh out loud.

Trooper Wood spoke carefully to me too, and when he did he smiled for the first time. It changed his stern face into a very pleasant one.

"How old are you, Annie?"

"I'm nine and a half, sir. Do you know where my mommy went?"

"Did you see her leave, Annie?"

"No sir," I said.

"Did anyone come to the door?"

"I was upstairs," I said. "Where'd she go?"

"I'm sure she's okay," he promised.

He went over to Veronica next, who was holding a small mirror and applying cherry lip gloss as if it were makeup. He leaned down to her.

"Where's your Mommy, sweetheart?" he asked with that same smile.

Veronica turned to Trooper Wood. "I don't know," she said with an exaggerated shrug and a cherry pout.

"Did she go somewhere?"

"Uh huh. I heard her."

"Is that a yes?"

"Uh huh."

"Was anyone with her?"

"I don't know."

"Did anyone come to the door?"

"I don't think so."

"It's very important."

But Veronica didn't understand, and the officer wasn't going to alarm her about her mommy.

Trooper Wood asked me about Rainbow then, who was now out limping in the creek, lapping up minnows. Had Rainbow been inside then? *Yes.* Had he been behaving strangely? *No.* Had he barked at all that morning? *Not that I heard.* Did he ever bark at all? *I guess, if there's someone he doesn't know.*

The troopers went to the neighbors next, which my dad had already done. They hadn't seen my mom either. All the police notes are still available because they don't destroy anything in cases like this one. When I went over the notes before the trial, I learned that our neighbors said we were new on the street and seemed to be a happy family (as if they would know), that we made sure our lawn was perfect (as if it mattered), and they said that they had seen no unusual cars in the neighborhood, no suspicious vans or anyone lurking. They never heard any quarrels from our house, but they said they were dismayed that we didn't go to church, not to any of them. That was pointed out more than once, probably because of my dad's book and my mom being a Sikh. We needed to pray more. Christian prayers. (Right.) But other than that one major flaw, they said we were always pleasant enough. (Thank you very much.)

Another thing I remember from that day is that my dad's parents arrived an hour after the troopers did. Grandpa and Grandma were Sam and Janet Taylor. They were alarmed by the police cars out front, and raced to the front porch as fast as two older people could. I remember my dad calling to them from upstairs where he was moving through the rooms again and again, looking for something, anything. "Something's wrong," he cried down to them.

"The state police cars!" his father shouted back.

"They're checking with neighbors. Sunny isn't here and she would never have left the girls alone. The door was locked too, which Sunny almost never does when she's here."

"Where is she?"

"Dad, I don't know! Just let me keep looking."

That was the third time my dad was going through the house top to bottom, hurriedly the first time, then a second time real calm-like, and now frantically. I later learned in my high school health class about going into shock when you see something awful or realize a rupture in your life is really, really happening. My teacher described how there might be a noise in your head like a rumble or a murmur, or like water just over your ears in the tub. She said that the sounds move with you and you might not notice them, that minutes and hours don't move the same so later you probably won't remember much. That's what happened to my dad because he couldn't remember a lot later. I heard him talking to himself as he went through the upstairs and then downstairs and the basement again. He went out into the yard, and even looked in the utility closet again.

He shouted to Grandpa Sam, "Maybe it's just a stupid reaction and there's a perfectly good reason, I don't know. Just watch the kids as we keep looking, will you?"

I remember that Grandpa Sam had brought a tricycle for Veronica and a big two-wheeler for me. He had put the bikes together himself at his store down in the City. His store was *Liberty Bikes*. It was on Lafayette, not far from The Village. It's still there, and he still runs it, an upscale store for the rich and status conscious. Grandpa Sam always claimed to have the finest and best-looking bikes in the City — touring bikes, off road and hybrid bikes, and the best technicians too.

Anyway, when Dad finally noticed the bikes, he thanked his father for the nice surprise, then told him and Grandma Janet not to let us girls out of the house, not for a second, not even into the yard. He didn't have to say it, but I knew he was afraid we might somehow slip away too and disappear into thin air like my mom.

Late that afternoon my mom still wasn't back and Trooper Wood brought in what he called a scent-dog to search for a cone of scent that could be Mom's. Rainbow started barking and Dad told me to put him in the basement. Then someone brought in a really big tracking dog that could follow particles that were heavier than air, like tissue and skin cells and other things that would have been left behind. There were a lot of traces of Mom on the property but none beyond it. Her car was still there, so she had been taken by someone or run off with someone. Or she was somehow still here.

In the living room Trooper Wood asked more questions of my dad while another officer took notes.

"You sure it was 9:45 when you went to the store?"

"I checked because my parents were coming around 12:00."

"Which store did you go to?"

"Mitch's."

"You're the doctor, aren't you? The one with the book?"

"That's right?"

"I haven't read it." Stone face, no nod of approval. "And it couldn't have been before 9:45?"

"No, I'm sure."

They watched my dad for any telltale signs. Too talkative or defensive. Too upset or angry. Not enough concern. Too demonstrative. Too cool. Arms folded. Arms open. Was Simon Taylor underplaying or overplaying his role? The notes say that Trooper Wood couldn't tell for sure.

The police checked Dad's new cell and the landline, and asked him politely if they could borrow his computer. There might have been some confidential things on there about his old clients, but Dad didn't care. He gave it to them right away. Mom's new cell phone was missing too. Records later showed that it hadn't been used since that day. As for Dad's phone, it had no suspicious activity on it, no calls to motels or escorts or a girl-friend, or practically anyone at all.

"What about friends?" the police asked him. Dad told them that they really didn't have many social friends locally, just colleagues and good acquaintances in the City. He was too busy writing and speaking about his book at conferences, and Mom was too busy with us kids and her doing everything.

The troopers also went to Mitch's Market to verify that my dad had been there. The store didn't have any security cameras, but the person working the counter said he thought he remembered my dad that morning. The fellow had been busy, though, and couldn't be exactly sure of the time.

Later in the afternoon Trooper Wood ordered the other two officers to put up yellow tape between the front tree and the post by the driveway. He said it wasn't really a crime scene yet, but it would at least keep others away for now. I was standing in the kitchen doorway as my dad watched them secure the tape. He was trembling and there were beads of sweat on his forehead. He pushed past me into the kitchen and threw up in the sink. I stood by him trying not to cry.

A new officer then arrived with a laptop, and asked questions to compile a biographical sketch of my mom—name, description, age, date and place of birth, interests, and friends. They didn't have to write down my mom's looks though. That was clear enough in the photos Dad had given them. Sunny Taylor was a stunner. Long, black hair, almost always braided. Skin a cinnamon tan. A freckle below the corner of her mouth, and a smile that would make you smile back at her. Dad told me once about when they were walking past a table by the market where a man was registering Republican voters, and of course Mom stopped to help the poor guy get over his confusion. It took some time, Dad said, and all the while the man frowned sternly at Mom and shook his head at her; but when Mom was done she smiled brightly at him, and he lit up and beamed back at her. It was that kind of smile.

Later that first night that Mom was gone, my dad and my grandparents were downstairs talking in hushed voices, and I got Veronica ready for her bath. It was my mom's job, but I was going to take over until she came back. I didn't believe she was really gone. I didn't understand anything at all.

I remember putting in Mom's lavender bubble bath as I filled the tub, then helping Veronica over the side and into the warm water. There were mounds of bubbles for her. I fashioned them like purple icebergs and clouds and swirling soft ice cream.

"Where's Mom?" Veronica asked me.

"She's away for a bit," I said. "She'll be back," I added, and helped her wash her chubby pink doll. I had brought a naked Barbie who was leaning back in the soap dish watching us.

"When will she be back?" Veronica wanted to know.

"Just a few minutes, I think," I told her, then washed her hair with no-tears shampoo and showed her how the naked Barbie could dive through the clouds and the soft ice cream.

My dad came in as I was drying Veronica off. Even though he was smiling, there was something awful on his face. He was bent over oddly like he had lost some bones that had made him straight. He was glad I had taken over and even had Veronica's PJs ready. He scooped us both into his arms and told me I was truly a big girl now, and he thanked me.

"We'll be together, tonight," he told us with a half-smile.

"Where's Mom?" Veronica asked again.

"Don't you worry," he said.

He took us to their bedroom, where I sat on the side of the bed as he tucked in Veronica on Mom's side and told us the story of the magic frog that lost her wand. That was mostly for Veronica, but it comforted me too. After the story he smiled and kissed Veronica five times on the forehead, counting each kiss as he always did because he loved Veronica and wanted her to learn her numbers. He came around the bed then and gave me a little tuck in too, and the same five kisses too.

"Is Mom coming back tomorrow?"

"I think so, baby."

"Where is she?"

"She'll be here, don't you worry. Grandpa and Grandma are here too, in your room. Everything's okay."

"The dogs scared me, Daddy."

"They were trying to help, and they're gone now."

"They scared Rainbow too. Is he okay?"

Rainbow lifted his head from the side of the bed and rested his chin on the blanket. Rainbow always slept downstairs. For the first time I wondered if someone was coming for me too.

Then Dad tested me with some spelling like he always did because he wanted me to get better at it. "How to you spell 'equilateral'?"

"E-Q-U-I-L-A-T-E-R-A-L," I said.

"What's another word for 'gigantic'?"

"Colossal," I said.

"You're really good, Annie. Can you spell 'colossal'?"

"Dad, that's too easy."

He smiled, though I could tell he was still so sad. Then he checked the window to make sure it was locked. He had brought in my princess night-light and plugged it in and turned it on.

"I'll be back in a few minutes and we'll all sleep together," he said.

"What about the stars, Dad?" He always told us a story, about Orion the hunter or maybe Andromeda the chained up lady. My favorite was Arcas, who was transformed by Juno into a bear and is still up there as the Little Dipper.

"Not tonight, baby." Then he went to the door and blew us lots of kisses. It was our routine, most of it anyway, usually with my mom there too; and that night my dad carried out the kisses with a special precision, as if they were the only thing that might hold our world together.

3

A disposition to perversions is natural to the human sexual instinct.
-Sigmund Freud

FROM THE INVESTIGATORS' NOTES

I went to Dr. Taylor for two years, and of course I bought his book right when it came out. He always knew the right questions to ask. He was happy and he made me want to be happy.
— Jane Whitson[1]

Dr. Taylor's book saved my marriage. Thank you Dr. Taylor!
—Jeffrey Hart[2]

It was a sex book. That's all it was. —Ginny Fields[3]

The guy's a freak. —Terrance Gibbs[4]

---

[1] Patient (police interview, November 3, 2005)

[2] Patient (missing persons interview, October 30, 2005)

[3] Neighbor on Mill Street(missing person's interview, October 24, 2005)

[4] Neighbor on Library Road (missing person's Interview, October 24, 2005)

MISSING PERSON:

SUNDAR SIMAR-TAYLOR

(AKA SUNNY TAYLOR)_

REPORTED MISSING: OCTOBER 24, 2005.

LAST SEEN: HOME, 9:45 AM,

DOB: 4/15/1970

AGE: THIRTY SIX

DESC: 5'8" BLACK/BROWN 130LBS

PLACE OF BIRTH: LAHORE, INDIA

REL: PRACTICING SIKH

PARENTS: ARJUN AND JASPIR SIMAR, LAHORE, INDIA.

HISTORY: LAHORE UNIVERSITY, AGE 23; CAME TO U.S. AGE 27. COLUMBIA UNIVERSITY –ONE YEAR, ART HISTORY; MARRIED. TWO CHILDREN — ANNIE AND VERONICA.

ORGANIZATIONS: ABALONE ALLIANCE GROUP. ALBANY WOMEN'S SOCCER. EARTH FIRST!

DISTINGUISHING MARKS:

1) SCAR ON RIGHT SHIN TO RIGHT KNEE.

2) TWO PIERCINGS IN LEFT EAR.

3) SMALL FRECKLE BELOW BOTTOM LIP

TRAFFIC AND CRIMINAL

14 TRAFFIC VIOLATIONS

2 ASSAULTS WITH INTENT TO CAUSE SERIOUS PHYSICAL INJURY.

VIOLATIONS OF PENAL CODE 120.05

Simon's sex therapy is brave and brilliant, and really breaks new ground in an age-old topic — sexual love. —John C Callaghan, Ph.D. American Therapists' Society

Don't know what's in it, but I never needed a book to do it. I mean, how good can it be? —John Wilson[5]

Simon is going to find Sunny, that's for sure. I know Simon. He'll never give up. He loved that woman more than anything.
—Dr. Samuel T. Bowers[6]

---

[5] Neighbor on Mill Street (missing person's Interview, October 24, 2005)
[6] Colleague & Practicing Therapist (police interview, December 4, 2005.)

4

**No psychologist who deals with the half-tamed
demons that inhabit the human beast, can expect
to come through the struggle unscathed.
-Sigmund Freud**

I'M AT UNION COLLEGE NOW, IN SCHENECTADY. It's not as fancy
as the schools my dad went to, but it's close to home, and Dad
really likes that. My friends here are into trendy things like computer animation and fashion design and international business.
Some are going to get rich in the market. Good luck. I haven't
told them that I've decided to be like my dad.

I didn't always want to be like my dad. He was *my dad*, after
all, and besides, for a long time I thought being a shrink was a
really dumb job. But everyone grows up. When I was fifteen my
plan was to do perfect cartwheels, be even more popular, and get
a lot of piercings someday. And I'd wear a red push up bra to
school like one of the other girls did. When I was sixteen my goal
was to dump my braces and be a famous writer who travelled to
wonderful places and met important people, mostly guys. I
didn't know that I was super smart and really dumb all at the
same time.

Last week I called Dad, and we talked for the first time in a while. I told him I had a surprise.

"Hey, I love surprises," he said.

"I'm going to major in psychology," I said.

"Really?"

"Obsessions and phobias, Dad, just like you did when you started out."

"That's so great, baby," he said, and I knew he was smiling. Then he told me that if I wanted to understand obsessions and phobias, that I had to start with Freud. He said Freud was the master who had laid out a roadmap for us, at least as much as anyone could.

"But you've got to be careful, Annie," he added.

"What do you mean, Dad?"

"Things stick to you, sweetheart. You be careful. Promise me you'll be careful. I don't want things to stick to you."

"I promise."

I told him that I'd already signed up for Abnormal Psychology and something called Cognitive Disorders. Now, after speaking to him, I've started reading Freud on my own, about phobias. I'll be ready one day.

I've already learned that there are all kinds of phobias, from the more common ones like coulrophobia — the fear of clowns, to the more exotic varieties such as ouranophobia — the fear of heaven. There's also eurotophobia — the fear of female genitalia. Hard to believe, but I guess it's true. Freud says that phobias are a result of unconscious conflicts inside us. The instinctual part of us wants one thing, mostly sex and control, and the moralizing part wants us to be sweet and good. So we repress the conflict, Freud says, and place it on an object — clowns, heaven, even female genitalia. Now we fear them.

Don't worry, I don't understand it all either. But I will.

Because I'm nineteen and a woman now, Dad seemed freer about explaining things to me than when I was younger. I told him I was writing everything down about what happened to Mom, and what happened afterward, and he was really open to it. "Maybe it'll be good therapy," he said. He told me that before he wrote his best-seller he was a lot like other psychotherapists taking on new cases as walk-ins or by referral, but that he wasn't all that happy with the way his practice was going because not enough patients came to him with their phobias and obsessions. People started listening to Prozac, he said, and didn't want to talk anymore. Patients came only with the usual problems, what Dad called "the maladies of a self-absorbed age."

Dad said that a lot of them were attractive women who feared rejection and middle-aged men wondering what it all means. Dad said he cared about them all, but more than once he wanted to get them into a room and politely tell them all to *just get over it, will you?* I know he was being open with me as a grownup woman because he told me that what the women really needed was a good three-day lay to convince them they were wanted, and the men ought to first get a spine and after that find a devoted wife who would do it the way men really want. *That's what it all means*, he said.

Yes, he was a Freudian. Of course my dad never said anything like that to his patients, and I imagine him trying to stay awake all those years as they mewled and whined on his couch.

What changed everything, he told me, was the day a patient came back after a month's absence and told him that he had hired prostitutes to talk to for his therapy. They were cheaper than my dad. But one of the prostitutes laughed at the guy and told him to get out. My dad laughed too. Then he told the guy to get out.

That was his last patient. He closed the business for good and went home to my Mom and me and little Veronica. Then he wrote his famous book.

I still remember how happy Mom was having my dad home with us. Of course my dad loved being home too, playing with Veronica and helping me with things like my hard homework (mostly math) and playing brain games with me and word games he'd make up right in his head. It took him a year to write his book, then another year for it to come out. Then four months for it to climb to the best-seller list. Suddenly Dad was famous.

Mom and Dad had met just fifteen months before I was born. Dad liked to brag that he hadn't chosen her. Mom had chosen him. It was one of her many whims, he always said, one of those *feelings* she had. I've learned that no guy minds being chosen. A lot of them are shy and insecure, and besides, it's every guy's dream to be singled out by a beautiful woman.

Dad liked to tell the story about that afternoon during lunch hour at the *La Sirene* restaurant in Soho, which was near where they each lived back then. Dad was sitting alone at an open window by the sidewalk and Mom was having a club sandwich near the bar. He didn't notice her glancing over at him and turning down offers from other men to buy her a glass of wine. Mom never drank. Not just because of her Sikh-religious thing. She didn't like what it did to her head. She was probably having her usual Sprite.

She later told Dad that she had a *feeling* about him that day, about that man sitting by himself over there by the window. Her *feelings* were usually right on. She had a *feeling* years before that she should learn Swahili and go to Kenya to work with children, and she had done it. The most fulfilling time in her life, she said, until I was born, and then Veronica. She also had a *feeling* about coming to America, and a *feeling* about studying in New York. Only once had her feelings not worked out. In her teens she had run off on a whim to New Delhi and married a rock guitar player. I guess it was like the way some Americans run off to Tijuana and get married for a week and then divorced. Dad said that when you're not yet twenty, almost every choice is disastrous.

That was his way of warning me, too.

Mom later said that her *feeling* on that day had been flawless. Dad hadn't exactly been looking, but yes, he was available. Mom could see that he was nice-looking, more than nice-looking actually, though not perfect looking, which was also just right for my mom. She guessed he was a doctor of some sort, yes definitely a doctor, but it was okay because he didn't have those soft urban looks that most doctors do. She later told friends that he wasn't too pretty either: *Hair too perfect, looks out of a catalogue. Freaking boring.* From across the room she imagined that he was quirky too, in the right ways, and not ordinary. That's what my mom had feared the most, marrying someone *ordinary*. Dad told me that whenever she said the word "ordinary" in passing it came off her lips sounding like a kind of dirty word.

Mom always said that looking across the room at the man by the window, something about Dad told her that he wasn't ordinary, and even if he was a little ordinary, still she had a *feeling*. So she carried her plate to his table and set it down. Dad was startled. He started to stand up but she waved at him to stay seated.

"Have you ever *giddha'd*?" Mom said.

He stared up at her. "Excuse me?"

"It's a Sikh dance. For special occasions. Like weddings or the birth of a child."

"Are you asking me if I'm married?"

"I'm just asking if you've ever *giddha'd.*"

It was unmistakable, even to Dad. She was coming on to him, this wonderful looking creature. She was entering his boundaries. And while he hadn't been *looking,* not consciously anyway, he told me that everyone is looking for the right person. And he's right.

Dad drew a breath. "I can't say that I have . . . whatever it is you said."

Mom repeated it then—*gii-dhaa'd*—speaking slowly and drawing out the vowels so he could follow it with her mouth. I guess it was kind of sexy the way she said it, and now Dad played along, saying the word too, and hoping it sounded as sexy as when she said it. But he said he stuttered on the *d* and the *haaa* came out too aspirated, like a cat hissing.

Mom told him it was perfect, which it certainly wasn't. He stood then and reached for a chair. "Please," he said.

She shook her head. "Will you *giddha,* with me? Right now?"

He looked around. There was no dance floor, not even any music playing above the chatter. I know Dad wasn't much of a dancer at all.

"We'll go somewhere," she quickly added.

"It's lunchtime," he said.

She gave him a one-shoulder shrug in slow motion. My dad finally caught on and gave her a slow motion shrug right back.

They left right then. His food almost finished. Her plate still on the table. They went down the street to a little coffee place fairly deserted after the morning caffeine rush. Some tables had been pushed aside for cleaning so he took her to an open spot on the floor. Nothing special was playing, something vague from the 80's that was slow enough for him to handle. She was already moving a little to it as he took her hand. Neither of them really wanted to *giddha*. Yet. They would save it for their wedding and the birth of us girls.

Dad said that after he took her hand they danced silently, wordlessly, a few inches apart. After a time he slowly turned Mom out and away from him in a little spin, still holding her hand and only letting her go so far, then pulling her back closer. They laughed, and soon they each relaxed in the other's arms, a bit sleepy-eyed, and unconsciously gauging the way the other felt, the right height difference, the subtle smells and movements.

"You're from India," he said softly into Mom's ear, as if answering a question she had asked him.

"Have you been there?" she asked.

"I hear they have big families."

"Extended families are big, but immediate ones aren't so large." A moment later my mom added, "How many children?"

"None," he whispered back.

"I know that. I mean how many do you want?"

"Two."

"Two?"

"And you?" he asked.

"Three," she told him.

"Oh, I hope there's some room for some negotiation there."

"Sorry, I'm afraid not," Mom said.

"I guess it won't work out then."

"Yes, a pity."

That's when Dad kissed her freckle for the first time, gently just below her mouth and then he kissed her full on her lips. But I know he wasn't at all like that, coming on so quickly. Mom was irresistible to him, that's all.

Some of Dad's friends told him Mom was too beautiful, and hinted that they thought she was a bit unstable. In their own ways they tried to tell him that he shouldn't marry her. That she wouldn't stay around. One friend came right out and said he thought Mom was a nutcase and that Dad didn't see it, or couldn't, or he didn't want to.

Of course Mom wasn't a nutcase at all. But there were some things about her that *ordinary* people wouldn't understand. Her whims, her little fancies. Her *dheaan* — her meditation. She would simply stop somewhere, pull the car over or maybe pause on the street to remember the Beloved One, and disappear into herself for a few moments. It could happen anytime, driving me to school, for example, and she'd just pull over for a few moments; and I saw it even in the middle of one of Mom's soccer games. She waved to be taken out and then retreated to a quiet place. And her seeing auras, or thinking she could, was a bit too much for Dad's friends. But Dad didn't care what they thought. He wanted Mom. I think it was in part because Mom trusted the world so much, trusted the world in a way that my dad didn't. She seemed to have a secret knowledge that everything will turn out perfectly in the end.

They *giddha'd* just six months later at their wedding, and again after I was born and when Veronica was born. Two of us, so far. I bet they were negotiating about the third. Then the money came in, and we moved to Windham. Then everything changed.

Dad said that the morning after Mom was gone, he woke up not knowing whether it had really happened or if anyone or anything would still be there, even the house or the neighborhood. He came down the stairs cautiously. Veronica was riding her new tricycle in a fast circle on the living room rug. The police were long gone and the yellow tape was sagging. Grandma Janet was on the phone to someone and Grandpa Sam was in the yard throwing a Frisbee for three-legged Rainbow. Everything was almost like it should have been.

Dad told me that he went right into the downstairs bathroom in case he threw up again. My mom, Sunny, had removed the door to the medicine cabinet when we moved in (a precaution I'll explain later). Dad said he waited there at the sink, leaning on it with both hands as he stared into the mostly empty cabinet shelves. After a time he put his hand over his mouth and started to squeeze his thumb and fingers together. He wasn't sure what he was trying to do, maybe slap himself awake or hurt himself so he could feel something, or maybe stop the vomit or a sob or howl.

Dad also said that sometimes he could sense things like Mom did; that particular part of her had rubbed off on him some. Standing in the bathroom that morning with his hand against his mouth, in his mind's eye he could see someone closing Sunny's eyes. He said the image repeated itself, the palm of a hand over both of her eyelids, closing them as a pastor would or maybe a surgeon. Again and again, and finally Dad had to use one of the tricks in his book to shake himself free of it.

Then he turned, and with a smile came back to Veronica and me.

5

**The mind is like an iceberg. It floats with
one-seventh of its bulk above water.
-Sigmund Freud**

OTHER NOTES FROM THE INVESTIGATION

Dr. Taylor explained that the word phobia comes from the Greek pho-
bos, *which means flight, or to make someone flee. He showed me his little trick for stopping my fears. I loved him for it.*
— Cynthia James[7]

*Simon was too much of a Freudian, sexual repression theory and all
that. He took it too far, way too far. That's where he went wrong.*
—William J. Booker, Ph.D.[8]

*I suffered from Samhainophobia. I could hardly even say the word. At
Halloween I would be absolutely terrified. Now it's all so silly. I can't
believe how his little trick helped me.*
—Name withheld on request[9]

---

[7] Patient, (missing persons interview, December 1, 2005)
[8] Practicing psychologist & colleague of Dr. Taylor (police interview, December 19, 2005)
[9] Patient, (missing persons interview, January 3, 2006)

During our first session Dr. Taylor told me — "Inside every person is another person deprived of what he wants." He wanted me to find that person. I never went back. The guy was nuts.
— Name withheld on request[10]

We are all mortal. We are all damaged. All of us.
— Dr. Simon Taylor[11]

Just reading the title of his book, I knew it was dirty.
— Emilia Cains[12]

There's another woman who's missing too. That's what I read. The guy really had a history. — Rev. Arnold Bowers[13]

---

[10] Patient (police interview, February 19, 2006)
[11] Excerpt from Preface of Dad's book.
[12] Neighbor (missing persons interview, December 9, 2005)
[13] Pastor of *Hope Restoring Church,* Windham, NY (police interview August 14, 2014)

6

**The virtuous man contents himself with dreaming
about what the wicked man actually does.
-Sigmund Freud**

THERE WERE SIGHTINGS OF MOM. She was on a subway in the
City. She was boarding a plane in Albany. A friend of Dad's spot-
ted her crossing the street in Boston, smiling her wonderful smile,
her long braid swaying behind her. Someone even secretly took a
picture of her at a restaurant in Philadelphia and then sent it to
Dad. The picture was taken from the side: Mom was sitting alone
in a booth with her coffee. The photo was slightly blurred, but
Mom looked composed and serene as if nothing had happened to
her.

I didn't know anything about those sightings back then. I
never even saw the photo until before the trial when I started
exploring everything for myself. It was in a trunk in the attic with
a lot of other things about Mom. Dad never threw anything away
if it was about her.

In the photo Mom had shortened her long braid, and the
freckle under her lip had been removed. And she was stirring her
coffee. It wasn't Mom. God, *Waheguru,* had given her that hair. It

wasn't hers to change. Her freckle was a gift also. She never drank coffee because she would not become dependent on anything but God.

Then it was six weeks and seven weeks, and then it was four months after Mom was gone. Then five months. The police search for her went on only half-heartedly now and with little hope. The *she'll be back* encouragements to my dad had tapered off and then finally stopped. When the phone rang it was Dad's agent or a telemarketer. Veronica turned three and graduated from chubby baby dolls to slender Barbie's. Rainbow was his usual self, limping around happily in the creek or bringing us a stick to throw. I was about to turn ten and was looking more and more like my mom. I still searched every passing car for her on the way to school. I was also a star student in my fifth grade class, and liked both of the twins, Kevin and Johnny Powell. I could tell them apart when no one else could. I was asking my dad questions each night about how my teacher, Mrs. Donaldson, got a baby inside her. It was confusing. Dad's descriptions and hand gestures about how the peeny and the vagi worked weren't much help at all. The Freudian shrink who had written a book mostly on the subject and who could talk about it freely with adults, fumbled and was red-faced in front of his inquiring daughter. I'm sure he wished that Mom were there to explain it girl-to-girl.

I was still waiting for Mom to come back.

Dad never stopped looking for her and never stopped following the discoveries of bodies. The woman found by a stream outside of Atlanta was the wrong size and coloring. The remains that turned up in North Carolina didn't have a DNA match. Bodies were appearing everywhere, it seemed to him. He was both frightened by the number of them and relieved that none were hers. At home he would point to one of the pictures of Mom and talk about her as if she would bound through the door any minute with her arms full of groceries. She was *gone*, that's all. That's the word he always used — *gone*, and never any of the other words: Missing. Strangled. Or worse. No, she was *gone*. *Gone* to the movies or *gone* to the City, maybe *gone* to visit her parents in India. She was *gone*. That was all.

Dad was waiting for her to come back too.

Right before the trial there were newspaper articles and even investigative shows suggesting all kinds of things about my mom. But I knew her from the inside, how tranquil and patient she was, except when it came to social inequities and damages to the planet. Mom was greener than Greenpeace, and I think now that if she thought it would have helped, she might have thrown herself into a volcano to save the rainforests. When I did my own investigations last year, I even found a clip of her on NPR smiling with other faces behind a line of phones. Pledge time. Sunny Taylor was pledged to everything good. The animal shelter. Child welfare laws. Clean air and water. She even saved batteries for recycling and of course marched for awareness of everything good and true. She ran marathons to show support for her causes. Mom was an engine of a woman going everywhere, doing everything. I know, because a lot of the time Veronica and I got dragged along.

My parents hardly ever argued. The only time I remember my dad even raising his voice was when Mom was driving too fast — *There are kids in the car, Sunny!* — and when she was arrested for assault — *You have a family! For God's sake, Sunny, you have a family!* But I don't recall any ill-spoken words that they couldn't take back, or the usual quicksand that couples step into. But as a kid,

I might not have picked up on it all back then.

I'm sure the usual pressures were there for them, but money wasn't one of them because of Dad's book and personal appearances. That left mostly the daily annoyances, the many small ones that always seem huge at the moment. I 'd heard my mom raise her voice in all four of her languages, mostly at the politicians on TV and of course the credit card people screwing up again, and one time at the manager at the courtesy counter of Nordstrom when we went into the City. When Mom raised her voice it didn't matter which language it was in. Sometimes she'd choose one that the other person couldn't understand at all. But she could have been speaking Martian and the meaning was still clear and beautiful for me to hear.

When I spoke to Dad last week I asked him if he could remember the last thing Mom had said to him. He laughed softly.

"Of course, Annie," he said. "I remember it very well. Your mom said, 'I'll kill you.'"

He laughed quietly again before continuing. "But the whole sentence was, 'Don't forget the Parmesan, Simon, or I'll kill you.'"

Dad was suddenly quiet except for a deep breath that I heard over the phone, not as if holding back from me, but as if holding something inside him. He was remembering her, and I thought he was going to cry. Dad then told me that Mom was standing at the door when she said it, and he had stopped and turned toward her on his way to the car. She wouldn't have killed him of course, and she said it with such a mischievous smile and a lifting of one eyebrow in what my dad said was a devilish way that he wanted to rush my mom back upstairs for round two of the morning. That's what he called it, *round two*.

Now that I'm older Dad isn't so squeamish when it comes to talking about sex with me, not like before, even a few things about him and Mom. Most kids don't like to think about their parents that way, but I know now that sex is just one of the body's many needs. According to my dad's best-seller, our minds really need it too. Sex is also supposed to be fun, though not so much for me yet. I'm not saying I'm scared or don't want to say *yes*, even though all my friends already have. I think about it, and I've had chances too. I've felt the sudden warmth and the hundred tiny levers turning in me. Since I was thirteen I've imagined it, like ancient voices in my head. I just knew it wouldn't work out for me yet. And Dad always said not to trust boys.

Anyway, Dad told me that *round one* had been just a bit hurried because it was Saturday and there was still so much to do before my grandparents arrived. But he admitted there had been enough time for the one thing that my mom enjoyed the most. I didn't want him to tell me what it was, and he didn't. I can imagine round one with just time enough to lie there afterwards, their sweat drying. It's nice for me to think about that. They deserved nice things.

But standing there on the walkway to the car, my dad knew that round two would be pressing it too much because my grandparents were arriving soon, and he reluctantly backed away, waving to my mom. "She had that look," he told me, "and the look said — *I love you like crazy.*"

I was too young to know anything about round one and round two back then, about what that meant. Adults knew though, and in the days after Mom was gone, Dad told everyone that unnecessary detail. The police too, even his parents. He was blaming himself. It was all his fault. He should have gone back.

Then Sunny would still be here. The police nodded politely when he went on about it; his parents looked down, embarrassed. Everyone felt sorry for him.

It's easy for others to see that Dad's guilt wasn't justified. But it's almost impossible to clear your head once you're trapped inside that confused mental cloud of what Dad called the "thought loop" or the "crazed maze." When you get like that you need help from the outside, and that's why even therapists have their own therapists. Dad's book wasn't just about his controversial sex therapy. It also covered some of his earlier studies — phobias and obsessions, especially his clever trick for dealing with these repeating thought-loops. But when Mom was gone, Dad was helpless to remember even his own methods which had been so helpful to others.

So to him, not going for *round two* was simply the unforgivable fact. He should have gone for it; I guess stepping back toward my mom at the door, taking her hand, leading her quietly past Veronica and me wherever we were in the house, and taking Sunny up the stairs, maybe watching her long braid bounce right and left with each step. I still remember what my mom was wearing that last morning: one of my dad's plaid shirts, blue and green flannel sloping over her shoulders and baggy jeans that I think would have slipped off in a second. They wouldn't have stepped into my mom's meditation room though, because it was sacred, kind of, and used only for that purpose. She was really firm about that. But maybe the second door down, the walk-in closet. That would have been even better. The rows of clothes above them would have muffled everything and made it all the more fun. I can imagine them laughing softly afterward like two kids who had just hidden some Snickers under the mattress.

I hope I'm not sounding too weird or voyeuristic here. I'm just being honest, and I like thinking about them still being together, that's all. Then the family would still be intact, and the near-perfect world we had together.

No family is perfect all the time. That's just for scrapbooks and Facebook. Mom and Dad were perfect in my eyes, and still are, but there were other problems. Mostly my grandparents. Grandpa Sam the Bicycle Man was a bully to my dad. I never actually saw it, but I could hear it in his voice when he spoke to my dad or to Grandma Janet. Even to my mom, sometimes. He was pretty old to me but still big with a thick chest and furry arms. He was kind of a loudmouth too, especially when bragging that his store was making so much money and that there was a four-week wait when you brought your bike in, and how people would pay double to have it done right away so they wouldn't have to find a place on the other side of town.

And Grandma Janet, how shall I describe her? Let me count the ways. Friendly. Warm. Mostly considerate. And forever beaming. Grandma Janet was also a God-Enthusiast. And I'm being polite. Grandma Janet was a Saint-in-Waiting. She had been raised a Catholic, then deserted to Lutheranism, fled to Presbyterianism, and next to something else before she returned to Catholicism; and now she assures everyone she meets that the Catholic churches are the only ones that God Himself visits on Sunday morning. Grandma Janet even started going door to door like the Mormons and Jehovah's Witnesses. It wasn't a Catholic thing, of course, going door to door, but she and some friends from church would take Amtrak from the City some Saturdays and go to towns like New Rochelle or Hudson and cheerfully ring doorbells and announce the location of the nearest Catholic church and tell people that if they made a sign of the cross using holy water it took seven years off their time in purgatory.

Grandma Janet was especially hard on my mom because of her Sikh faith. Grandma Janet would say things like— *I bet you don't even have real saints.* Or— *My Savior died on the cross, so what did yours do?* Mom told me once that whenever Grandma Janet said things like that, she'd just remember *Waheguru,* the Sikh word for God, the Loving and Compassionate One; and remembering *Waheguru,* Mom would just give Grandma Janet that wonderful Mom smile.

Then there were my other grandparents, Arjun and Jaspir, the ones in India who I'd never met but who I later learned kept pushing Mom, their beautiful daughter, Sundar, to leave Dad and come back to the Punjab with Veronica and me. It must have been a big pressure because Mom loved her parents so much. I'm sure there were other cultural pressures too, but she would never have left us and gone back.

I've lived half my life now without my mom, so when Dad and I talked last week I asked him to tell me some things I didn't know about her, some things I would have missed because I was too young or maybe because they seemed too personal back then. He paused a long time on the phone.

"Come on, Dad. Just simple things. The things that made you love her."

Through the phone I could hear him sigh. "There really isn't anything too personal, Annie," he started. "I loved that only one of your mother's ears was pierced, the left one. It was pierced twice, as you know. It was so like her. She didn't like symmetry. Only God was perfect, she would tell me." Dad continued about the freckle below her lip, the hourglass birthmark on her left shoulder blade, and then he suddenly stopped.

"What are you thinking about, Dad?"

"Just how I'd just watch her as she moved through the kitchen or was hanging up wet towels by the tub, even while she was asleep. Sometimes I'd see her from the window when she was in the yard; when we went out I'd notice other men looking at her too."

"That's pretty normal."

Dad made a sound I couldn't decipher. "I know about men," he said. "Sweetie, I know about men and the terrible things they can imagine."

That was another warning to me.

"But what about *personal* things, Dad?"

"Well, you won't remember that she stayed up late for Leno. She never recorded him because she wanted to laugh at the same time the rest of the country did. It just wasn't the same the next day. Sometimes I'd catch her sneaking Lucky Charms from you in the morning before her own bowl of *Special K,* and sometimes she'd have a Hostess cupcake for lunch, a 'diet cupcake,' she'd inform me when I found a smear of chocolate on her somewhere. But I knew Hostess didn't make anything diet."

"Dad, that is so sweet."

"You didn't know about her one cigarette a day," he continued.

"No! Mom smoked? You're kidding."

"Just one. She'd take a Marlboro Light and go out on the porch while you kids were napping. But it was a mental habit for Sunny more than a physical one. She'd sit there with my Red Sox hat on and put her feet up, and just watch the wind in the trees. She would never wear the hat on backwards, but always with the bill toward the front, like it was supposed to be."

There were other things about mom I still remembered and didn't have to ask. That her almost-British accent was difficult for people to place. Though she was from Punjab originally, she could have been from a lot of places. Not because she was cosmopolitan-like and could fit in anywhere. It was just that there was something "everyplace" about her, like the curve of the earth. That's the only way I can explain it.

If Mom wore perfume it was the tiniest drop behind her right ear. She told me to always be careful with perfume because women overuse it and men don't like that and won't ever tell you. She played soccer on a team each Sunday. She was a vegetarian most of the time. And she couldn't stand New Agers because they always said: *Well, I guess it was just meant to be.* For Mom, nothing bad was meant to be. And if something was bad, you worked to change it. Mom had more bras in her drawer than shoes in her closet. And she had a penchant (a new word I've learned) for purple cars and old ones with running boards. Mom had even spent a year in Kenya inoculating children from measles. See what I mean? An engine of a woman.

Mom's killer looks surprised you. She seemed petite at first, but then up close she was suddenly tall, with raven hair in a long braid that fell all the way to her waist. Mom knew how attractive she was, but I don't remember her ever being vain about it, puckering in front of the mirror or checking how her bottom looked. She just shrugged it off and said, "Annie, God is the Decider about those things, *Waheguru*, the *Wonderful Teacher* who alone is the cause of everything." In other words, if she was beautiful, she couldn't take credit for it. I think that made her even more beautiful in people's eyes.

Freud didn't believe in religion. He called it an illusion, a universal neurosis. That's one thing about Freud I'm not so sure about yet. I'm going to look closer at Sikhism one day. If my mom said that it was true, then it's worth a look.

Dad came back with the Parmesan cheese just forty-five minutes later. Not the Parmesan in a can, or Mom might really have killed him. (No, not really.) He came back with a wedge of Parmesan, and everything was the same, or almost the same, because the door had been locked which was unusual when my mom was there. She trusted people. No one would hurt us. Veronica was cooking in her plastic kitchen. I was horsing around upstairs. Mom's music was still playing, Dad remembered, something soft by Eric Clapton. The dishwasher hummed, and Rainbow was standing at the back door to go out.

But there was no sign of Mom.

Dad reminded me that they had polygraphed him the next day. He said that he didn't resent it. He said the police often believe the husband did it, and they were only eliminating him as a suspect. They had to be sure. There were four polygraph tests in all. He passed them all with flying colors.

Dad also told me that at one point when the police were there, Grandma Janet the Saint-in-Waiting piped up about my mom. *Such a strange religion*, she told them. *Who are those Sikhs anyway? Not Christians, that's for sure. And their saints aren't even real, did you know that?* Then she started in on Mom's color, as if it wasn't mine and Veronica's too. Sand? Cinnamon? She was sure the neighbors were prejudiced. *She's not black, you know, and that's good*, she told the police, even saying it to Trooper Wood. Grandma Janet could be oblivious. Grandpa Sam had to break in and tell Grandma Janet to shut her trap. No such luck. *And she doesn't look Hispanic either, which is good too. But you know, I'm sure the neighbors are wondering if she's a* real *American, and asking each other if anything has gone missing.*

See what I mean. Not sensitive. I'm sure Grandpa Sam the bully and Bicycle Man was cringing inside and rolling his eyes, waiting for the police to leave so he could have a *private consultation with Grandma.* That's what he always called it, or a *heart-to-heart.*

But Dad did tell me that the neighbors were curious about Mom after we moved in. They might see her in the yard or strike up a conversation with her at the market, and they would eventually, oh so politely, ask her. "I'm Indian," she would explain, knowing they would think of the reservation or Geronimo or Tonto. They would nod and smile vaguely, and Mom would have to add, "From India," and they would say, "Of course."

Six months after Mom was gone something happened, something that would later change everything. That was in April 2006. I even remember that exact day because it was right after my tenth birthday and Dad was scheduled to give a talk at a psychiatric conference in St. Louis. He didn't have to go. We didn't need the money and he didn't need to promote his new book. But he had been scheduled for a whole year of conferences before Mom was gone, and Dad always kept a promise. He didn't want to disappoint. I think that some conferences even changed their topics just to include Dad because of his controversial sex therapy. He was a drawing card. Everyone thinks about sex and they love to hear about it, probably due to our natural voyeuristic tendencies. Maybe it's more; maybe it's an obsession that's natural to us. And everyone knew Dad would give a great talk. He was in demand because he was answering the public's basic craving by talking about sex in direct language; not only that, my dad was easy

going, funny. He was sympathetic to all questioners and all questions.

If I had known what was going to happen at that conference,
I would have stopped him from going or tried to stop time, freeze
it if I could, or have done something else, maybe faked a disease
or jumped out of a tree and broken my leg so that he wouldn't
walk out the door to go to the conference and say what he did.

Anyway, we didn't know it then, but going off to that St.
Louis conference was the end — or the beginning of the end — for
Dad and Veronica and me.

7

**Sexuality is the key to the problem of
psychoneuroses, and of neuroses in general.
-Sigmund Freud.**

It was a conference mostly on phobias and obsessions, and they had included Dad, not so much because of his background in phobias and obsessions, but so he could talk about his dynamic sex therapy. Whenever he gave a talk, Grandpa Sam the Bicycle Man and Grandma Janet the Saint-in-Waiting would drive up from the City to take care of Veronica and me. Dad would be gone for two days at a time, sometimes three, never more. It was mostly fun when my grandparents looked after us, except for having to go to confession with Grandma, and every evening having to listen to her read from the catechism about purity and obedience of faith.

As I said, that conference in April of 2006 was the beginning of the end. But we wouldn't know that until eight more winters of terrific snowboarding and beautiful white layers of snow piled on pines, and after eight more wonderful springs of slow warming and sudden buds and flowerings had passed. That's when the reporter from the *Post* went digging for dirt on my dad and discovered what Dad had said at that conference.

There are photos from the St. Louis conference. In one, Dad is climbing the stairs from the lobby of the Renaissance Hotel where he was to give his talk. He is heading to the conference room level. The photo is an odd one because it shows Dad just as he's reaching the first landing of the staircase. The camera is somewhere behind him, so it captures both Dad's back and his front reflection in a mirror that covers the wall in front of him.

In the photo it looks as if Dad is raising his hand to slap his thigh. In fact, that's exactly what he was doing. It might seem odd, but it was one of the techniques Dad had taught in his practice. You do his little trick — slap your thigh and laugh at the thing you're afraid of — and you break the thought loop you're about to go into. It's kind of stupid sounding, I know, but it worked for Dad and for thousands of others, and that's all that matters.

Part of what I'm saying is that my dad had an issue too. He had an apprehension. A concern. It's called catoptrophobia. A fear of mirrors. Catoptrophobia is from the Greek word *catoptro* for mirror and of course *phobia* for fear. My mom didn't know about it when she married him, but she knew soon after, of course, and Veronica and I knew too.

Mirrors never totally lost their power over Dad. Even today, after the trial, he still has to use the slap and laugh trick sometimes. It's not so absurd if you think about it. If you encounter the thing you're afraid of — ghosts, darkness, black cats or mirrors, breaking the thought loop is a way of disrupting the crazed maze you're about to step into. First you catch yourself, and then you slap your thigh and laugh. It's a way of admitting to yourself that your fear isn't rational, that it's absurd and even possibly stupid. And yes, slapping your side and challenging your phobia by laughing out loud at it can be embarrassing and silly, even to yourself. That's the point. Do something to shift your focus away from the thing you fear. Being embarrassed will do that. It shifts your thoughts away from being afraid of something, to being afraid that you look foolish; and looking foolish often outweighs the phobia itself, at least for a time.

If you have a phobia you can try Dad's slap and laugh trick and see for yourself if it works. I don't have a phobia, but I take Dad's word for it, and the word of so many who benefited from his technique.

Dad almost never had to do the slap and laugh thing at home because Sunny had removed the mirrors from their bathroom, and mine and Veronica's too. We each had our own hand mirrors tucked away, and there were tall shrouded mirrors on the back of our closet doors. Dad shaved with an electric razor each morning without a mirror. Mom always checked him for any missed spots. She also checked him to make sure his tie was straight. After she was gone, I took over those duties, and did so happily.

Yet depending on backlighting and the time of day or night, a window at home or on a storefront could become mirror-like. Dad would do his little trick and then steel himself and smile into his reflection. It took a lot of effort sometimes. If a mirror surprised him, he could go into a kind of partial paralysis and become confused. I'd see Dad stagger then, and turn sideways and slap his leg and have a hard time turning back around to stare at his image. When he challenged it, he would always smile.

It was a great smile. Mom used to say that whenever the corners of Dad's mouth turned up, his eyes looked so merry. She called them "Santa Claus eyes." Mom had a great smile too, even better than Dad's, and a great laugh except that she sometimes snorted. If we were watching something funny on TV, Dad would roll his eyes and point sideways with his thumb at Mom, and say, *Your mother.*

There are other photos from that day at the St. Louis hotel. There's one of him standing at the reservations counter and another of him getting into an elevator with polished-brass doors to go to his room. Another photo shows him approaching the Washington Room where he was to speak. There's a large placard outside the double doors. I had to get out my magnifying glass to read it. It had Dad's name on it alongside a black-and-white photo of him smiling, Santa Claus eyes and all. The placard read:

WASHINGTON ROOM
EASTERN PSYCHIATRIC CONFERENCE
ON PHOBIAS, OBSESSIONS,
& DYNAMIC SEX THERAPIES:
9:30 AM.
DR. SIMON TAYLOR PRESENTING
FROM HIS BEST-SELLING BOOK:
YES, TWICE A DAY
(THANK YOU)
-A GUIDE FOR COUPLES-

I learned later that Dad always skipped the conference breakfasts and the long opening remarks. He preferred to arrive at the time of his talk and avoid the unnecessary chit-chat. Then, after the talk, he would spend extra time answering everyone's questions. When he entered, the plates with partially eaten pastry and fruit would already have been cleared and everyone would be waiting for him at their linen-clothed tables with coffee or tea.

I imagine him now as he enters the Washington Room. A woman at the lead table notices him immediately. She stands and goes to the microphone to get the audience's attention. All eyes go to Dad. He is about to speak. The room is filled not only with a hundred or so therapists. His adoring public has paid their money too. Everyone wants to hear about sex.

Dad is introduced: Johns Hopkins University; University of Pennsylvania studies in cognitive psychotherapy; Private practice in New York City; Expressive therapy, interpersonal therapy, narrative therapy, Freudian psychoanalysis; Best-selling author.

Although his book, *Yes, Twice a Day*, was loved by the public, it was mocked by many of his colleagues. From the day it came out the needful public raved about it and by extension about Dad. They said his book was insightful with astoundingly curative sex-therapies for everything from leukophobia (the fear of things that are white) to ecdemomania (an obsession to travel). They loved what he said about sex as a remedy to so many things, and loved when he explained what Freud had meant about "death."

But Dad's colleagues ridiculed the book. It was a sham, they said, and a mockery of any legitimate sex therapy. It was simplistic, warm and fuzzy. Give the stupid public what they want. It was an embarrassment to the field. And based on what research?

Dad told me once that right after the book came out there had been groans and even some catcalls from his colleagues when he rose to speak. Some privately told him it hadn't been smart to walk away from his lucrative practice. But those groans and catcalls stopped after Mom was gone. Then his colleagues were all sensitive and cordial when he spoke.

I imagine him now as he takes the stage in St. Louis. He hears the murmurs first, then some uncertain stirrings. A few people are pointing, and then they politely applaud out of respect or pity, he doesn't know which. That's followed by a louder applause and even some cheers to encourage him. I know that Dad is thinking of Sunny, but he will have to push her from his mind for now.

I see him taking out his papers and placing them on the podium. He scans the room and the participants. Dad is ready with a frank and compassionate talk that's intended to heal and renew and provide sexual insight that will bring others the relief they have sought for so long.

Dad looks up and faces his audience again. The corners of his mouth rise to the applause, his Santa Claus eyes thanking them for the warm welcome. He does not know that what he is about to say, a few of his off-hand remarks, will later be read and reread, analyzed and investigated.

Then Dad begins his speech in his frank and wonderful way. He does not know that what he's about to say will destroy us.

The truth is sometimes like that.

8

Every normal person is only "normal" on the average. His ego approximates to that of the psychotic person in some part or other.
-Sigmund Freud

I had pogonophobia, which means I couldn't be around anyone with a beard. Talk about limiting your life. But the slap and laugh trick did it for me. Now I'm happy, and married. No, Hector doesn't have a beard, but I can go anywhere now. Dr. Taylor made it all possible.
— Terry Cole[14]

I went to him every week, and he told me the same thing over and over — that inside every person is another person deprived of what he really wants. That should have been my clue to get out. He was weird.
— Linda Wilkins[15]

He could have beaten the polygraph if he took a lot of valium beforehand. As a psychiatrist, Dr. Taylor certainly had the access.
— Wilson Call Certified Expert Polygraph Examiner

---

[14] Former patient, (police interview, September 12, 2014)
[15] Former patient, (police interview, November 17, 2014)

When they found the other girl he'd killed, I guess that was the clincher. Then they really had him.[16]

Maybe she wouldn't give it to him twice a day. That's motive.
—Howard Singleton[17]

---

[16] Neighbor, name withheld on request, (police interview July 19, 2014).
[17] "Man on the Street Interview" by reporter Sandra Whitlock for WRGB TV, Sunday, November 5, 2014.

9

**Sexual love is undoubtedly one of the main
things in life; and this union of mental and bodily
satisfaction is one of its culminating peaks.
-Sigmund Freud**

Excerpt from My Dad's Presentation:
(Recorded by Ted Wilson
of the St. Louis Post-Dispatch, April 19, 2006.)
(Long applause)

DR. TAYLOR: *Thank you. Thank you.*

*I especially want to thank the Council for inviting me to this lovely
city today. I see some friends here.* (Applause) *And, well, some not so
friendly colleagues.* (Laughter) *But I thank you all, and I hope we'll
have a helpful meeting of minds today.*

*I'm only going to speak briefly this morning so that we have more
time for questions at the end. Most of you have read my book. I'll restate
some of its main theories for those who haven't read it and to refresh the
memories of those who have.*

(Long pause)

*Do you know about the stars? Of course you do. I learned about the
stars when I was a young man and worked in the fields in the daytime —*

we raised corn and beets and sunflowers and some other things – and I would look up, but I never saw any stars. Based on that alone I could have concluded that stars don't exist. But they were there – we know they are always there – because at night we can see them. Even at night we see only the smallest fraction of all the stars.

Why? Because here's the rule: The light that is closest to us seems the brightest even when it isn't. This is obvious. It's because the closest light obscures the greater brightness of the many other lights behind it.

The closest light to our earth is the sun. Inside of us, inside our minds, I mean, the closest and most visible light is our consciousness. When we're awake, our consciousness seems to be everything. Usually we think that our consciousness is us. We think we are choosing and deciding and doing everything through our conscious decisions. But we now know – through depth analysis – that our consciousness is really a veil over what we call the unconscious – our individual unconscious – which is always operating much more deeply. In fact our unconscious is hidden from us, just as the stars are hidden from us in the daytime. That's my point. The unconscious is hidden, like the stars, but it's there – right there – and it determines most of our motives and actions.

Now you are thinking, 'Yes, yes, Simon, we're aware of that, and about dreams too, and psychoanalytic theory and the rest of it. Get on with your sex therapies.'

I will. My point is this – and I must thank my wife Sunny for the insight, bless her; and, as always, once an insight is realized it becomes so obvious – my point is, that even the unconscious must have its own – can I say it? Okay, I'll say it. Even the unconscious must have its own origin. I mean, where does our unconscious get the drives which propel our instincts and actions? Where? Where?

So the unconscious must have its own source too. Do you see? Are you with me?

You see, our unconscious has a goal, and that goal is what Freud calls "death." But Freud's "death drive" must be rightly understood.

You want me to get to my sex therapy, and I will. It's coming. I'll hurry up.

In analysis we try to dig down into the unconscious through talk therapy or art therapy, visualization, dream analysis and more. We want to somehow wake up the unconscious or wake ourselves up so we can root out the reason why we do something that might be hurting ourselves or others. Usually we think the cause is something that occurred in childhood, but we have to admit that we rarely find that deepest source.

So, here's my question: Why not skip all those therapies? Why not skip the unconscious all together? Or almost all together.

I really mean it. Why not? I don't think anyone's ever thought of that before, though I believe Freud was onto it in his much misunderstood "death drive."

What I'm saying is that sometimes we can skip dealing with the unconscious. Blow right past it, to its own source – death. Yes, death.

The thesis of my book is exactly that. The way to getting back to the true source, more primal than even our unconscious, is – and now I'm going to say it right out, plain and simple.

Two words: **The orgasm.**

Have you ever worried during an orgasm? (Laughter) *Thought about the VISA bill that hadn't been paid? Wondered why the neighbor never cut his hedge? Why the politicians did what they did? Have you ever been afraid of anyone during an orgasm? Or angry at anyone? The answer is obvious. No!* (Laughter)

So, why not? The first reason that pops into our heads is that it's because this great pleasure of the orgasm is so all-encompassing that it distracts us from all worries. But that's not really it.

The real reason is because at that special moment in which time seems to go on forever – and we wish it would (laughter) – at that moment we are fully and totally concentrated. We are focused all the way to our center, to our very core. We are focused in a way that we are never focused at any other time. If someone was watching us during those intense moments it would appear as if we are in a panicked frenzy; yet inside us we experience a kind of stillness. Complete stillness. Complete focus. Yes, a kind of death. In those trembling moments of the orgasm we seem to be snatched out of time. No lingering pains from childhood, and no projecting of a worrisome future. For we are lost somewhere. Or I should say that we are wonderfully found somewhere – in this very still and quiet place. It is a joy that is a part of weeping.

This is what Freud meant by his "Death Principle." All tension leaving the body. In that still and quiet place we are momentarily returned to a time before us, to our inorganic origin.

During our conscious hours we are usually troubled about a hundred things, silently talking to ourselves when we don't even realize it. But at the moment of what I call that special culmination – the orgasm – all our problems, our worries and self-talk are gone. Aren't they? We are carried away, though not away from ourselves. We are actually carried back to ourselves. We lose our daily selves. In fact, in those long moments, we are no longer our daily selves at all. But we are somehow still there.

So, this stillness, this inner quiet we experience in those moments is also a terrific satisfaction, and not just a bodily one. It is our quiet return to where we came from, the place before life – that's Freud's "Death Principle" – and where our core has been waiting for us all day, just like the stars are always waiting there even when we can't see them.

As I say in my book, even my "slap and laugh" technique for phobias and obsessions is just a method for our consciousness to startle away the paralysis that accompanies a phobia. But it takes more than consciousness to be wholly healthy.

So, this special culmination, the finale of what we call the sex act, is much more important and necessary than we have understood up to now. It is a gateway to nearly all psychological healing.

Let me ask you something else. Have you seen two raindrops sliding down a windowpane? How they move in parallel, and then suddenly — what happens? They slide together, don't they? They unite as if pulled together like magnets. My wife, Sunny, showed me that during a sudden storm at our home, how the two raindrops suddenly converged because they are of the same element and from the same source. From the same cause. That's what happens during this special culmination. In those timeless instants the focused life-forces of the two lovers become one.

I will summarize by saying that this return to unity is the real *reason we seek orgasms again and again. We seek this quiet place even more than we seek the tremendous physical pleasure it gives us. During these special culminations we are momentarily delivered back, not only to the womb, but even before the womb.*

That's why I say we need Twice-a-Day therapy — two orgasms each day, to obliterate, at least for a time, our daily selves, all that we have thought we are; and to let us remember our very cores. Twice a Day leads us home. Twice a Day reminds us at the deepest level that we already *are home. Not once a day, but the sheer and wonderful exhaustion of twice a day. And. after the orgasm we experience a silent* Thank You *that we feel, to ourselves and to our partner, a* Thank You *for returning us to our source.*

That's my book in a nutshell. (Applause)

Thank you. Thank you. (Applause) *I don't mean for an orgasm.* (Laughter)

Now, I'll take your questions.

QUESTIONER #1: *When you began your talk about the stars, you mentioned working in the fields and raising crops. We don't know anything about that part of your life. Were you raised on a farm?*

DR. TAYLOR: *Oh, a personal question. Okay. No, I wasn't raised on a farm. I grew up in New York City where my father had a bike store. He still does.*

QUESTIONER #2: *When did you work in the fields, sir?*

DR. TAYLOR: *I guess that's a long story. I'll try to make it short. Well, like a lot of kids after high school, then and now, I was confused about everything. Nothing made sense to me. Like many others I felt like I had been thrown into the world at birth, and I just couldn't sort it all out. I think if you asked your own patients whether they feel like they were thrown into the world at birth they would laugh with relief because you've given them the words to express what they've felt all long. That was me, too.*

But I didn't join the army like a lot of kids who don't have a clue. I dropped out and joined a commune. I'm not going to say where it was, because it may still be functioning, and I don't want anyone barging in on it. It was a foolish place for me to be in the short time I was there. I was what you might call a Latter-Day-Hippie (laughter), thinking I was escaping the frictions and fears of the world, hiding in a remote place with others who were escaping too.

But when I got there I found that there was really no escaping, because I had to take myself along; and that was the real problem — me. (Laughter)

The commune was a great place, in theory. It was full of work, food, and sex. But the work was hard and the food wasn't very good. At least the sex was great. (Laughter) *And frequent.* (More laughter) *It made* up for the work and the food. We'd even go around naked sometimes just to show how free we were.

Of course we weren't free at all. We were just trying to be free. Trying to find a way to be free. But what we were doing wasn't working.

So, that's when I considered how the stars were above me all the time, even in the day. And that's how my interest in psychiatry began . . .

-End of Excerpt-

10

**The ego represents what we call reason and sanity,
in contrast to the id which contains the passions.
-Sigmund Freud**

I WAS EIGHTEEN DURING THE TRIAL, and had just started early here at Union College, but I dropped out of my classes to be with Dad. I was at the courthouse every day. I took care of Dad the best I could at home, and of course I took care of Veronica and Rainbow too. Anything I could do, I did. Grandpa Sam the Bicycle Man and Grandma Janet the Saint-in-Waiting were also there a lot. I always listened carefully when Dad met with Mr. Aireys, his lawyer. His lawyer didn't like me being there. Once he even called me a "pain in the ass" for asking so many questions. His irritation would start off slow, and build up.

I think Dad should take the stand, I'd say.

Shouldn't you be at school, Annie?

I'm just saying what seems reasonable, Mr. Aireys. Why can't I say things?

Because I'm Simon's attorney, not you. There's nothing for you to say. Your father will listen to me.

But there's no evidence against him. That's what you said. He should take the stand.

My clients don't take the stand, okay?

No, it's not okay. You think Dad did it, don't you?

I never said that, Annie. He's my client!

Yeah, but it's in your voice! You think he did it!

Things like that. Each time Mr. Aireys would give me an exasperated look and glance over at Dad. I would sometimes be on my feet at the end of our verbal sparring contests and so furious that I'd have to leave the room. But Dad always insisted that I be there. I could say anything I wanted.

Though I'd dropped out of college during the trial, I still had some time to pick up Freud and try to understand him; I was hoping Freud might help me understand what happened to my mom too, or at least why. Freud wrote a lot about how people have secret sexual needs that are at the bottom of their neuroses, and how even what people think are their normal actions are really a result of deeper sexual desires. That's what the word "libido" means. It's Latin for *I desire.* Anyway, Freud is all about sex and aggression. That's all of us, he says. But we scrub our faces clean before we go outside, put on our masks, and no one knows about our fantasies and aggressive needs.

When I think of myself I don't see a lot of that, I mean raw fantasies and aggressions. About sex, if it matters, it's mostly the same random desires that my friends talk about at school. Sometimes they joke about doing slutty things. Nothing like that for me though, but a few times different things crossed my mind that I'd like to try one day when I'm ready. I mostly think about my family and falling in love with the right guy, a guy like my dad, and being swept away by soft and sweet things, nothing really harsh.

Maybe I'm hiding things from myself about how I'd like it. Freud was honest though. He even admitted that when he was young he had sexual thoughts about his mother, among others. So maybe I'm holding back and not admitting everything to myself yet.

About aggression, I only feel it against those who libeled my dad and attacked him relentlessly on the news shows and in court. But I have a special anger for one person: His name is Will Halverton.

Will Halverton found the speech Dad had given years before in Saint Louis. He found it in 2014, nine years after my mom was gone. At the time I was finishing up high school. I had just gone out with some grabby guy who I dumped, and some of my friends were going Goth or getting into drugs. I wasn't exactly a goody-goody, except when it came to boys. I worked hard at Carvel Ice Cream after school where I had to wear a frilly-pink apron. The owner said I drew in business. It was mostly guys. The owner said it was my smile, but I knew that wasn't it. I always remembered the way my mom was modest about herself, so I tried to be too, and I remembered what my dad always said about not trusting guys. But I couldn't wait to get out of high school and start college.

Will Halverton worked for the *Post*. He was what they call a stringer, though he called himself an investigative journalist in his articles about my dad. Halverton wasn't even trying to find out what happened to Mom. He wanted to be the next Woodward or Bernstein by getting something dirty or embarrassing on someone famous, something that would reveal the person to be a fraud or a cheat. That's the way reporters work. They can't write a great book that helps heal people, but they can destroy someone, or try to. It's easier to destroy than to create something wholesome and good.

He destroyed my dad.

I remember the phone ringing almost every day for a while, and my dad listening and then simply hanging up. I asked him what the call was about, and he said it was nobody or a wrong number. I learned later that Dad had heard that someone was looking into his past, digging through the footnotes in his books, examining his old talks and even questioning his friends and colleagues. Dad didn't want any part of it.

Once when Halverton called I was the one who answered. Halverton asked if he could come out and speak with me when my dad was away. "No!" I shouted into the phone. Then he said we could meet someplace private, like at a restaurant. "Just five minutes," he promised. "You'll see, just five minutes." I told him to get lost. I didn't quite say it that politely. I hung up.

Later, I told dad.

"Annie, people in the media, they don't have a story unless it's something shocking. They make their living by ruining people's lives."

Dad waited for my response. I waited for him to go on.

"They dig for dirt until they find something."

"What could they find?"

"Or they make something up. Look, things can be misunderstood, Annie. That's what I'm worried about. Let's not help him, Annie."

"About Mom?" I asked.

"I don't know," he answered with a shrug and a sad shake of his head.

But Dad wasn't telling me the truth.

All that time and I still missed my mom as though she had been taken from me just the day before. Other times I felt like I never had her, like she was a wonderful dream and all I had left were some lingering, slowly fading images. I remembered her eyes, brown and slightly oval, and their striking alertness, the mysterious richness of her skin, and how great she smelled after a shower, even after a soccer match, all sweaty in the front and back as she hugged me hard. I remember her actually spanking me once, baring my bottom and letting me have it — three smacks that didn't hurt much except that it was Mom who was hitting me. I cried about that more than the smacks. Then she sat down on the floor next to me and cried too.

I had been going through her dresser that morning as children do, pulling out clothes and trying them on, some stockings, her bra and other things, just to see how they looked on me. I was about six, and we were still living in the City then. I put her things on the best I could and then went to find her so she could see me all grown up. She was in the kitchen, and I just stood there with baggy hose and her bra that hung down on one side. I had Dad's Red Sox hat on like she sometimes did, the bill facing the front. I wore a little smile as I waited for Mom to turn around. She finally did. At first she smiled at me and almost laughed, but then she seemed startled and even scared at something. She came toward me quickly. "Annie, you can wear anything," she said, "anything, but ask Mommy first, and don't go through Mommy's things. People have *personal things*. Don't do it. *Please*, don't do it." She grabbed me then and turned me around. The loose hose fell away from my bottom and that's when she smacked me there three times. I was startled and scared, but mostly because Mom seemed scared at something too. I started to cry. That's when she collapsed around me and clutched me and began crying with me. Then we were laughing and both of us saying we were sorry. Then we were eating orange gummy bears and still laughing for some reason. But I understood that her things were *personal*, and I wasn't to go through them. Now I better understand why.

Girls know about crying but I don't think guys do, how it's like ice melting—something hard and cold suddenly warming and washing away the sadness. Guys don't have words either. They just have hands and eyes and a brain somewhere, and of course they have their protrusion that presses into you when they try to hug you or they get you in the back seat. But they don't have tears or words. Maybe guys just stay hard and cold. Maybe they can't let go of the ice.

But I have both—tears *and* words. Mostly tears now. Even during the trial I was so sad at times that I thought I'd never stop crying. I even heard Dad crying too, alone in his room sobbing quietly. He wasn't like other guys. He knew a lot about tears. I went in without knocking and put my arm around him. I kissed him five times on his forehead like he used to do, counting to five. He smiled then, and composed himself. He asked me to help him make dinner. "Frozen turkey again," he said, and then laughed. He pulled me closer and kissed me on my forehead five times, and smiled into my eyes. We would make it, he was telling me. In the end everything would be all right.

He couldn't have guessed how far from the truth that was. Nobody could have guessed.

11

**The tendency to aggression is an innate,
instinctual disposition in man.
-Sigmund Freud**

IT HAD TO DO WITH THE COMMUNE. That's what Will Halverton found in my dad's talk, and then he wanted to know where the commune was and what Dad did when he was there. Dad never said where it was located, but some of his old friends from high school or some relatives knew. It wasn't hard for Halverton to figure it out. And he did.

The commune was in Northern California, not very far from a town appropriately called "Weed." Mount Shasta is there too, and a ski park, and a national park, as well as a lot of lakes and the Pacific Crest Trail, which is a popular long-distance hiking trail that goes from Canada all the way to Mexico. The area has snow-capped peaks and some of the land is very rich.

All those years and Dad had not mentioned the commune even once to me, not once. I don't know if Mom knew about it; maybe she didn't. People have secrets. Everyone has secrets; I know that now. Or maybe Dad had told her a little about it. But Dad was a professional when he met her, and a lot of things people do when young they'd rather forget.

May 15th 2014: That's when Halverton's first piece came out in the *Post*. Everyone at Windham Central was talking about it. I asked Dad what it was about, and he said not to worry about it but to focus on Mom. Mom was still the issue. He hadn't let her go. But then he told me a few things about the commune and I researched it during the trial. I also watched the numerous investigative shows like *Dateline* about Dad and Mom that started running after Halverton's other columns appeared.

I learned that the commune didn't have a name. That's because the commune members back then thought that names are so *capitalistic* that having one would be selling out to *The System* because a name would somehow separate the commune from nature, just like all the towns, cities, and communities had already made themselves separate. That was the whole problem with everything, they thought. If you have a name, then you have a border, and if you have a border you're divided, and everyone really should be one big, huge, gigantic *One*. No boundaries between people and nature, no mayors or anyone in a uniform or anyone owning private property. No "this is mine" and "that is yours." Marriage is a kind of border too, because others are on the outside of it. That's separation. Separation is bad. Money is bad too, because some people will have more than others. So in the commune, there was no money. You traded things. I'm assuming that everyone worked for everyone else's good, and of course slept with everyone — twos, threes, fours — bodies all heaped in a bed. Lots of love.

You had to be there.

That was after the hippie craze that started in the sixties was almost over, but young people were still dropping out and turning on. They wanted a simpler life. Peace and love. Experimentation and drugs of course.

No flush toilets in the commune, though. That would have done it for me.

It's hard to not have boundaries. I feel my body as a kind of boundary that contains *me* and not some other person. Sometimes my body is particularly attracted to, let's say, that guy over there and not so much to this other guy over here. It's normal. Even scientists can't explain how chemistry like that works. I don't think they ever will.

When I try to think about it, how attraction works, I see that it's more than the unconscious working. There's something else too, maybe the flesh itself scouting around, sniffing, then pushing outward or drawing into itself, literally trying to duplicate itself, conceive another person; first through an anxious and tense body and then an anxious deed in an empty parking lot or the cab of a pickup truck, kisses and steam and almost always lies. Maybe that's why there's so much violence around sex and why it's so different from love.

Just writing this about this—violence and sex—now I can hardly breathe because my mind is racing ahead to that moment I figured out what happened to Mom. It was all so clear. I should have known. But I have to slow down here. I don't want to get there yet, my mind lurching to the end. I don't have the courage yet.

Mostly I don't want to be there all alone again.

I didn't ask Dad about why he was at the commune, but one afternoon he sat me down at the kitchen table and said it was time to talk a little. He didn't say a lot, but quietly, and hardly looking at me, Dad told me about when he was a kid.

"I hadn't fallen into the drug scene in high school, Annie. At least not much. Mostly I just needed to get away."

I knew he meant get away from Grandpa Sam and Grandma Janet.

"I took up hitching," he went on. "Lots of kids did back then. People actually picked you up when your thumb was out. Not like today."

Dad told me that he was standing on the side of a road somewhere in Nevada with his backpack on and his thumb out, smiling and waving at the cars as they passed. He got picked up by some people in a van, and they took him to the commune with no name.

When he got there he found that everyone was proudly calling it the No-Name Commune, because No-Name had become its name. I think a lot of things didn't make sense back then.

It's hard for me to imagine Dr. Simon Taylor being there, the refined doctor from the City who married Sunny and raised me and Veronica, and who spoke nationally and bought a new red Saab convertible almost every year. After the investigation shows aired I asked Dad more about it.

"I was there for about ten months, is all, Annie." He even dug out an old picture of himself to show me. It was a black-and-white snapshot, though I'm sure his bandana was red. His hair was so long I couldn't believe it was him. No beads in sight though, no bong either. Dad said that he hoped I'd have more sense than he did. He told me that they all worked so hard there, and everyone quoted Jesus or Buddha about love, or Karl Marx about how capital is dead labor and landlords reap what they never sowed. There was no division of labor between men and women, he said, because women were exactly the same as men, except that the women somehow wanted lace curtains to put up on the windows and they were the ones who kept the wood floors neatly swept.

That reporter, Will Halverton, calculated when my dad was at the commune; then he went out there to see for himself. He went out there in early 2014, but by that time the commune didn't exist anymore. It had died out for some reason in the mid-nineties. Most of its members disappeared into separate homes, got separate bank accounts, separate lovers, and I guess separate bongs, though some of its former members still hung around Weed and the surrounding area.

Halverton worked hard to get in touch with them, and somehow gained the confidence of some of them; that led to even more people coming forward with information about the commune, and more things about Dad.

I remember one of the investigative shows that I stayed up late for. It was a repeat from earlier in the day. I waited until Dad was in bed so he wouldn't know I was going to watch it. That was right before the trial started. The reporter for the show was one of those pretty, short-haired brunettes with a deep voice and a perpetually worried look that made you think the next thing out of her mouth was really going to shock you. But mostly that show was about commune members *remembering* the good old days, trying to make it seem like they had been some famous lost tribe and not just a bunch of naïve kids huddled on some remote tract of land warding off the heat and cold and bugs and the prickly windblown rains. First the TV cameras scanned the grounds which looked like a hundred acres or so of scrub and farmland, and then the pretty brunette reporter started in with the interviews of former members. It could have been a TV drama with famous actors disguised as heavy-set shopkeepers, businessmen, middle-aged wives and even hicks with missing teeth. Quite a bunch. One guy who ran a self-storage place — Elbourne, he said his name was — took the reporter around the grounds and pointed to where there used to be tomatoes and peppers and eggplants growing, and other things too, including, of course, marijuana. Elbourne told her that drugs weren't forbidden. Nothing was forbidden, except selfishness.

Elbourne also led the crew inside some of buildings clustered together at the commune's center and made from cheap unpainted wood and bricks and shingles that the members had gotten from the communities around Weed. It looked like there were no private rooms at the commune, just large living and sleeping spaces, a small dispensary for the occasional farming accident, a tool building, and a large room for cooking and eating which was also where the food was stored. Most of the time, he said, there were sixty to ninety No-Name members and a number of dogs that belonged to everyone. He pointed out that each building had a wood-burning stove for the winter, and there were kerosene lamps and also some electricity which he said they were *sharing* from a nearby power line. Each building also had an overhead light and a plug for electronics if anyone wanted to play records from the capitalistic world outside. No radios. No news. It wasn't forbidden, but there was simply no need for it. Everything was as self-contained as possible.

"It was our little attempt at Utopia," Elbourne said.

Dad had called it that too, *our little Utopia*, but he added that much later he learned "U-topia" is the Greek word for "noplace."

Funny.

On the show, the pretty brunette reporter also interviewed a guy name Charlie Dawes who was tall and heavy now with a beard that looked like a bird's nest. He ran the Weed Alehouse and he couldn't remember Simon Taylor at all by name. Hardly anyone could remember anybody by name, because when you joined you got a new name like the Indians did. Charlie said there was a Cloud Woman and a Butterfly and an Elk Man there, and I imagine also a Kicking Bear and a Great Mother Spirit too. Turns out Dad's name was Zebra. That's what Charlie called Dad. No one could remember how he got the name. Pretty silly, though.

Like Charlie Dawes, Elbourne and the others remembered Dad only as Zebra, and told the reporter that almost right away they knew he wasn't like them. Zebra was selfish. He liked girls for himself, and one time after a new girl arrived, Zebra tried to have her all to himself.

The girl's commune name was Morning, which I think was actually a pretty nice name. Zebra was jealous, they all said, even when others just looked at Morning. But jealousy wasn't allowed because everybody had to share. If you didn't share, you were a greedy capitalist and had come to the wrong place.

"Do you remember her, Dad?" I asked him one time during the trial. We were making lamb chops and string beans. Dad sat down on the kitchen chair with his head lowered.

"Barely, now," he told me.

"Was she nice?"

"She was very pretty and sweet . . . but not as pretty and sweet as your mom, that's for sure." He was lost in thought for a moment. "It was a very strange time, Annie."

I can't imagine my dad in love with anyone but Mom. It was probably just body-attraction, though maybe he had really fallen for her. Anyway Elbourne and Charlie Dawes and the others remembered that once Dad had even gotten into a fistfight with a guy when he saw him leading Morning away, probably to have sex. Zebra ran over and shoved him. The guy was surprised and asked Dad what was up. That's when Zebra hauled off and hit him, and they tumbled on the ground, Zebra swinging at him and hitting him with sticks even when he was down. Everyone ran over and stopped them because the commune was a peaceful place for people who wanted love and harmony and mellowness.

No one could remember the other guy's real name, but his commune name was Snow Goose, or just Goose. They couldn't remember what happened after the fight, whether Goose and Morning finally went off to have sex or not. But they all remembered what happened the next day. They were a bit wary when they talked about it to the reporter; their expressions grew worrisome because they remembered that nobody had called the police or any authorities to report what happened. The No-Name members didn't want anyone to know because then *the establishment* would come snooping around including cops and detectives. So everyone agreed that if anyone asked, they would say Morning had left, just like so many others who couldn't take the free spirit of commune life or were homesick or just moved on. Maybe they thought that what happened to her wasn't a big deal. Everyone dies someday, and maybe they thought she was safe now with the Great Unbounded Spirit or something.

I wonder what they were thinking when they found her. They were supposed to be peaceful people living in a peaceful community. But if Freud is right when he says that aggression is innate, inside us, then we can't move away from it—from ourselves—not even if we're living in a far-off commune. I'm sure the commune members weren't sitting around reading Freud, but maybe some of them considered that the reason they needed to live in a quiet and peaceful place was because there was something inside them that was working in the opposite direction. Or maybe they knew that aggressions are natural, just like the commune was natural, and they expected bad things to happen sometimes.

When Halverton did his own investigative work—this was just before the TV shows—he dug deep into Morning's death and probably had to bribe some of the commune people. They told him that they had gathered together to bury Morning on the evening after they found her. They walked a distance into the hills, chose a nice spot and took turns moving rocks and digging a deep hole. A group of them had already washed Morning's body and wrapped her naked in a nice woven blanket. All they had left to do was perform a little ceremony, and then lower her into the ground. I imagine them saying something generic, a boundary-less prayer that incorporated all religions and spirits and everything natural and good.

Anyway, they just buried Morning after the small ceremony. Dust to dust. It was all very organic, very natural, the usual cycle of life.

Except for the way she died.

12

**Suffering which comes from our relations to
other men is more painful than any other.
-Sigmund Freud**

WILL HALVERTON DISCOVERED THAT MORNING'S REAL NAME WAS
Christy Jones. Christy was nineteen, the same age I am now. She
was from Greenville, South Carolina and was smart and pretty.
She had a swimming scholarship at Duke, but after a blow up
with her parents right after high school, she ran off to lead her
own life.

Christy travelled the country with her thumb out like a lot of
kids did back then, eventually making it to the West Coast. She
kept in touch with her parents though. She called from pay
phones to tell them she was okay and happy. She was learning to
play the guitar and wasn't smoking pot. She told her parents not
to worry about her. But then they didn't hear from Christy again
for some months and that's when her parents grew really worried. They filed a missing persons report and went looking for
her.

Her parents even hired an investigator who somehow tracked
her to California and eventually to the No-Name commune. The

guy showed her picture around, but everyone told him that Morning, or Christy, had left some time ago, and that no, they couldn't remember much else about her. The investigator believed them and moved on to other dead ends.

Though Halverton had gone to Weed just to get dirt on my dad, now he started asking about Christy Jones, too. He figured it would be a pretty sensational article apart from my dad's story. And it was:

WHAT HAPPENED TO THE
PRETTY HIPPIE-GIRL CHRISTY JONES

What the No-Name members liked talking about most was the good old days, which were the best days of their lives, they said. Other than the fight between Zebra and Goose, no one could remember a cross word exchanged at No-Name or an unhappy day or any problem at all other than the winter weather and the summer bugs, which they all struggled through bravely. Times had been hard, but like soldiers who fought side by side they remembered it all with great fondness. It was such an unforgettable time, they said: a great and harmonious Utopia they would always cherish. They were proud that it was what had formed them, what made them who they were today.

Will Halverton wasn't stupid. He knew that a lot of their stories simply weren't true. It wasn't that the commune members were lying. The past gets exaggerated, and with years of embellishments, the legends of the commune had grown so much that a lot of the stories were now probably just folklore and grand myths. So he needed to find one person who remembered it as it really was — warts and pimples and leaky bongs and all.

He found that person. Her name was Sally-Ann Harkness.

She remembered everything.

13

**In abolishing private property we deprive
the person of his love of aggression.
-Sigmund Freud**

SALLY-ANN WAS STILL QUITE HIPPIE-LIKE when Halverton drove up to her little house on the edges of Weed. There were pictures of her in his article showing her with long hair that was naturally graying. After years of going braless she didn't seem to mind that nature was finally having its way. Yet she was still very pretty. Sally-Ann Harkness had a nice smile and unstooped shoulders. In the pictures, she looked right into the camera. I liked that.

Sally-Ann said that during her commune days her name was Dancing Swan. I don't know how she could keep a straight face when someone called out, *Hey Dancing Swan, why don't you dance your body over here?* Sometimes when I read about that period I feel like I missed something important. But Dancing Swan?

Sally-Ann said that she'd always loved cooking, even when she was living at the commune. And that's what she was doing now in the nearby town. She was an all-around cook at the Weed golf course and sometimes at the tiny Weed airport that she would hitch to. People still picked up hitchhikers around there. Sally-Ann hadn't married though she said she was now monogamous. She had become more politically active than she was in the old days, actually running for the state senate once as a Green. Everyone in town seemed to know and respect her.

Sally-Ann's memories of the commune seemed clear and balanced and she remembered Morning, or Christy Jones, very well. She remembered Zebra too.

"Oh, Zebra? Yeah, he was very bright, always polite, and a real hard worker. *A very, very hard worker,*" she emphasized. "Zebra would often eat the evening meal at the same table with me and Morning. Zebra helped everyone out. Oh, and he was the biggest reader there, some tossed-out classics he'd find in town. He also read the great novels, and a lot of other things too, I remember, even Shakespeare and Euripides."

That sounded like my dad.

As for Christy Jones, besides regularly eating the evening meal together, she worked with Sally-Ann planting corn and digging an irrigation line and even building a new communal latrine. Sally-Ann also said she had slept with Christy. They were just experimenting, she explained, adding that they liked holding each other more than the other stuff.

Sally-Ann described what Christy looked like when they found her at Black Pond. That's what they called it because the underground spring was so deep that it made the water seem real dark. "I'd seen some others running up the little hill toward the pond, so I ran and joined them," she said. "Zebra had found her. He found her at the edge of the pond."

Sally-Ann said that Christy's head and shoulders were submerged in the shallow water, her feet on land, with her arms thrown back over her head in the water, as though they had been held there.

"It looked like her neck was broken, though we didn't know because we'd never seen a broken neck before. It looked like her hands were tied with rope. At least that's what I thought at first. But it was really a thick kind of metal, like heavy wires. Like some kind of homemade handcuffs," she said.

Obviously someone had come onto their grounds and done this freakish thing. Nothing else was conceivable. Certainly not one of *them*.

"The next day some members left the commune," Sally-Anne said. "And we knew that we'd have to be more vigilant and protective of each other, now. Our tranquility and love would always survive."

When the *Post* ran pictures from back then all the guys were bearded and scruffy, and really thin too. Some of the girls weren't wearing any tops, just walking around clothed in nature's grace. There's one photo of a blond girl, really quite pretty, and maybe that's Christy Jones. A lot of the girls there were pretty. They ran a picture of my dad too, carrying what looks like a sack of seeds and waving to the camera. Great smile, even back then. He might be in some other pictures but I can't really be sure because some of them are grainy and out of focus, and with long hair and skinny bodies the guys looked a lot alike. There was one picture in which I recognized a very young Sally-Ann walking next to the blond girl who I thought might be Christy Jones.

Halverton figured he had something big now, so right away he contacted Christy Jones's parents and told them what he'd uncovered about her death. They flew out immediately. Mr. Denny Jones was a contractor bigwig, and he quickly arranged for an excavation team. The police got involved then too, and Sally-Ann Harkness had a lot of explaining to do, not just about where they had buried the body but also why she had been silent about it for so long.

Apparently Sally-Ann was her usual truthful but irreverent self. "It was the commune's code back then," she explained with a shrug. "We weren't going to get eaten up by *The System*." But she admitted her involvement only after her attorney assured her that the statute of limitations on failure to report a murder had already lapsed. A long time before.

I didn't have to have been there to imagine Sally-Ann leading the excavation team this way and that, stumbling over rocky ground and overgrown scrub with tools in hand, thinking it was here, then over there by that clump of bushes, no, dig here, no, I think it's closer to those trees; yes, the horse flies are huge, and they're hungry, especially the green ones that really hurt when they bite you, so be careful; yes it's been so long, maybe over by those rocks, no, that's where we plowed, so it must be farther up where the soil is darker.

Then something triggered Sally-Ann's memory and she was sure of the exact spot. They dug again. It wasn't long before they found the tattered woven blanket Christy had been wrapped in, and then discovered the rest of her.

My mom had been gone for more than nine years when it came out that Dad had been one of the people at the commune, and about how Christy died. Everyone knows that times change and the next generation can never figure out why the previous one wore the clothes they had or listened to that awful music or danced the way they did. But being a hippie, that was too much, even for some of my father's colleagues who were about his age and were surprised and dismayed. The sales of dad's book didn't drop off though, and he still had his speaking engagements.

Up until then hardly anyone was thinking of Mom, but I hadn't forgotten about her and of course Dad hadn't either. There were still no leads, no clues at all about what had happened to her. But Sally-Ann Harkness had told Halverton that when they all went running up to the pond it was Zebra, my Dad, who was leaning over Morning. He had just found her like that, Dad had explained to them. Exactly like that. He didn't do it. And he didn't know who did it either.

The articles ran the usual way, with wording like it's all so suspicious, like others at the commune *knew* who it was all along: *Zebra had found her. Zebra was right there leaning over her. Zebra denied any wrongdoing. Zebra was selfish, and a brawler. Now Zebra's wife, Sunny, is missing too.*

Suddenly Dad was in the news again, and that was enough to have the police take a second look at him as a suspect in Mom's disappearance. He'd already passed the polygraph test a number of times, so you'd think he would have been totally cleared. But he had a violent history now, and people were saying that no one else could have taken Sunny Taylor away. The troopers no longer believed he had gone to the store for Parmesan; they no longer believed what he had said about "round two."

A few days later I was walking home from school with Veronica when I heard Rainbow going crazy, growling and snapping, and saw Dad outside tying him up to the tree. The police were there with a search warrant. There really wasn't any new evidence, so I don't know how the police talked a judge into it. I guess the police were pretty persuasive. The cops had brought a number of vans and were presenting a paper to my dad. When they saw Veronica and me coming up the walk they said it would be best if Dad took us to the library or somewhere else for a while.

"This is our home," Dad announced. "We're not going anywhere."

"Sir, we're asking you not to interfere. If you do, you'll be arrested. All of you."

Dad was angry and that made me scared because I'd never seen him angry like that before.

They searched the whole house this time, not just the rooms and closets like they had done years before when they were looking for Mom. I don't know what they expected to find so many years later, but now they went through all the drawers and cubby holes and everything on each shelf. They brought a special light, and looked at every piece of furniture downstairs. They opened every trunk and piece of luggage in the attic. They searched all the boxes and bags everywhere and didn't find much except the usual personal things. They even found some things of my Mom's and Dad's still in the nightstand drawers, marital fun things I guess. Dad hadn't thrown them out. Mom was "gone," was all. Around the corner, out for a bit, and Dad was still waiting for her to come back for round two. When he found out the police had taken their things from the nightstand he became even angrier because someone might try to embarrass him by leaking it to the newspapers.

But the nightstand stuff never came out. That's not what mattered to the police. What mattered was what they found in Mom's meditation room. The police were just finishing up when Dad and Veronica and I returned hours later. The officer in charge came out of the house and held up something inside a plastic evidence bag.

"These yours?"

"Never saw them before," my dad insisted.

"Right," he said dismissively. "Found them in the little middle room. White dresser, second drawer, under some stuff."

"I'm telling you they're not mine," Dad insisted again. He looked over at me and Veronica. "They aren't mine," he repeated. "Annie, I don't know what's going on."

Dad accused the police of planting things, saying they had a vendetta against him, and that it was all a surprise to him, too. I remember being angry right along with Dad. But I knew that something about Dad seemed odd, like he wasn't telling the truth, even to me.

14

**No one who has seen a baby satiated from the breast
with a blissful smile can escape the reflection that this is
the same expression of sexual satisfaction in later life.**
-Sigmund Freud

Excerpt from
YES, TWICE A DAY
(THANK YOU)

Please understand that twice a day is not a retreat. It does not compensate for anything going wrong in your life. — page 55

*Those culminating moments are always the same, yet always new.
— page 151*

To an outsider it looks like life's panic, all shivers and moans and shrieks. But to the insider, all is quiet. All is still. — page 170

You must not hesitate to gulp those moments down, those special culminations that drain us fully. All tension leaves the body, all disquiet and distress; the flying hours are gone, and we are still for a time, inwardly still, in the very heart of flesh. — *page 194*

So practice 'twice a day.' Practice it every day. — *page 241*

Practice makes perfect. — *page 280*

15

The madman lives out his dreams when awake.
-Sigmund Freud

I HAVE TO STOP FOR A MINUTE. Getting this far is hard, and I'm not sure it's good therapy after all. Dads are supposed to be the ones who come to the school auditorium when you're all costumed-up as a tree or a pink fairy; the ones who patch up booboos and tell nighttime stories; the ones who bring home the bread. Dads are supposed to know everything in the world and watch out for you, warning you about others. Dads can be fierce when they need to be. Dads are safe. Dads are more distant than moms but they are just as loving. Dads don't make mistakes. And Dads don't have strange looking handcuffs hidden away.

That's what the police found: handcuffs in a blue box. There were two pairs in the box. A third pair was missing, because according to the box three pairs had been shipped. The handcuffs were an unusual type—slightly oval with three hinges, and they had some weird serpent-like etchings on them.

That they'd found them in Mom's meditation room was really odd. It was a special room just for the one purpose. Mom was very clear about that. Nothing but meditation was to go on in there. That was her place, her *private* space, unless we wanted to join her when she meditated. Even after she was gone it was *still* her special place.

I trusted Dad, but that night while heating some sauce and microwaving some frozen ravioli I couldn't stop the questions from repeating in my head. If the handcuffs really were in the house, I didn't know why they were there. And if Dad *did* know about them, why would he have kept them all those years after Mom was gone? It was confusing. Even if he *didn't* know about them as he said, and even if he *didn't* do anything to Mom — which I knew he didn't — it still looked bad. If Dad *did* know about them, he must have known that someday someone might find them. Maybe he was afraid to throw them out because they could be found in the trash or at the dump. Or maybe it was something else. A vendetta, just like he'd said.

The same questions kept spinning round in my head as I went to the silverware drawer to set the table. I looked up at the window that was darkened by the night and saw my reflection. I was shaking, and had to use Dad's slap and laugh trick to stop it. It worked, but the laughing made me feel stupid and then sad. I wanted to know the truth. I was old enough to know the truth. But I was afraid to ask Dad because he'd already said they weren't his.

When I think about someone having handcuffs I think that that person is either a police officer or into S & M. I don't know a lot about sadism and masochism, mostly just some of Freud's theories. But I've overheard my friends talking a little about S & M, and I've seen some raunchy videos I've come across on the Internet. Sadism is when you like to hurt others and masochism is when you like to be hurt, though Freud says that masochism is really sadism against yourself. I also know that there's sexual sadism and nonsexual sadism. Watching people in pain is not pleasurable to me, and I don't see how it can be pleasurable to be in pain. They are opposites. I never once had a hint that there was anything like S & M going on in our house. Not that I would have known everything my parents did at the time my mom disappeared. But it was just so very, very unlike either of them. They were such gentle people. The police didn't find anything else in the house that pointed to S & M; no whips or ball gags like I've seen on the Internet, or whatever other paraphernalia those people use. I've never understood why someone would want to be all tied up in a leather costume and strung tight with pulleys and ropes. It's a strange fetish, and I don't get it. I think that people who enjoy pain, on any level, must have a major personality disorder, which neither Mom nor Dad had. Dad was never interested in dominance. He was trying to stop the mental suffering of others, not create it. Mom was always trying to fix the world in her own way. Both were always kind and loving to Veronica and me. I couldn't believe it went on in our home.

Besides, the pair of handcuffs they claimed they found in our house was pretty tame compared to all that stuff on the Internet and other things people sometimes do, even humiliating things that I don't have to put down here. But if the handcuffs were Dad's, they could have had only one purpose, and that really scared me. Unless there was some other reason that I couldn't think of. They were an uncommon type that I've never seen on TV or in the movies, not like police handcuffs which are round and have a chain between the cuffs. Besides being a little oval and having the weird dragon etching, they were connected by three tight hinges so the person can hardly move in them at all.

I have to take a breath again, because my little book is getting me terrified all over again. But maybe that's what therapy is supposed to do. Maybe it's supposed to be like that primal scream remedy where you experience all your pain at once and let it out in one primitive howl so the trauma leaves you alone.

It's not working. I remember how I kept asking myself — *Could Dad have done something to Mom?* The answer was — *No!* I didn't want to think that back when Mom was with us, Dad had been so burdened that he went over the edge. He's too kind of a person, too even-tempered, too generally happy. Even after Mom was gone Dad always seemed basically happy or maybe pretending to be. He kept me and Veronica going, even if he was falling apart. Yet, then I had to ask myself — *Who else? Who could have done it?* Nobody. I couldn't think of anybody at all.

And now I'm living it all over again.

After the handcuffs were found everyone was seeing Dad in a bad light again. When Christy Jones had been strangled and drowned with a broken neck, her wrists had been tied with thick wire, ". . . like handcuffs," Sally-Anne had said. Jealous Zebra had been the one who found her. Now the police had discovered handcuffs at our house. And Mom had disappeared.

They brought Dad in for questioning again. He couldn't understand how those fragments added up, and his lawyer couldn't understand either. But Dad didn't get a lawyer until a week later, after more damage was done. Nice going Dad.

The police took a long time *interviewing* Dad, asking what happened to the third pair of handcuffs and what he'd done with all the other S & M stuff he had. I saw some parts of the interview during the trial, and the whole interview later when I did my own investigating. They had to release it.

"I don't know anything about them," my dad told them over and over. "You planted them. Jesus, you guys are really something."

"Oh, there's more Simon. You wanna hear more? We got DNA evidence from the Christy Jones site. And guess what? It's yours."

"Right," Dad said.

"Think we planted that too?"

"Except you never took my DNA, so it's obvious you're lying. You guys are amazing."

But they *did* have his DNA. They had found a few strands of his hair on some clothes in a closet while they were searching our home, and had sent them to a lab. They had Mom's and his both. Apparently something at the Christy Jones site was traceable to Dad having done it, or at least that's what they wanted him to believe.

I'd seen the good cop-bad cop routine on TV, but this was for real, with one officer badgering my dad and lying all over the place while the other was on Dad's side and looking for the simplest solution to it all, just trying to understand what happened to Christy Jones and Mom so he could *help* my dad.

"Simon, you said I could call you Simon, and thank you for that, but if you had a fight with Sunny, well, you know, we've all had fights with our wives so we understand how that can be. It can get out of hand sometimes. It happens to all of us, and it's understandable. Unintentional, we know. The handcuffs and the other things you had, we know they can be fun for role playing sometimes. We know something happened. We just want to know where Sunny is, Simon, and what you did to Christy Jones. We can help you then, and this'll all be behind us, finally."

Things like that.

Dad was too smart to say much, but not smart enough. I watched as the good cop tried to butter Dad up about how great his book was, and what a fine and lovely family he had. That's when he made the mistake of saying my mom, Sunny Taylor, was a *real looker*, and hadn't Dad been fortunate in that department?

That's when Dad exploded. I had to turn the tape off because I knew what was coming and didn't want to see it. When the good cop told him that my mom was a *real looker*, Dad had thought he was insulting her, like he was saying she was a hottie or something. In the next instant Dad was up and pummeling the guy to the floor. He laid the officer out pretty good before the other officer jumped on Dad and some others rushed into the room. Even then, Dad kept swinging at the policeman, swinging in the air as they pulled him off and forced him to the floor and held him down. Now he was under arrest for assault of a police officer. He was booked and placed in a cell.

Great.

The next morning the police brought in two detectives who specialized in questioning murder suspects. Sanchez and Brewer weren't exactly Mutt and Jeff, but they were pretty close. And of course they did the good cop bad cop again. Sanchez started by telling my dad that they already knew everything that happened to Christy Jones and my mom, and that they even had proof.

"Look, when we searched the house the first time we didn't find anything, Simon, not even the usual pornography most people have. That's good for you. But we know that back then you'd been using the library computer way over in Hunter to go online."

Hunter is a small nearby town with a branch library, and we're talking before cable and satellite were available in our outlying area. So everybody had dial-up at best. They wanted to know why Dad was driving all that way to Hunter just to use their dial-up over when he already had dial-up at home.

"You even passed another library, Simon, a closer one, to get to the one in Hunter."

So, why, Simon? Why?

I didn't know either

Dad shrugged helplessly and told them that he simply liked the town of Hunter, which he did. I remember him saying a couple of times how if we hadn't moved to Windham, we would have moved to Hunter instead because it was a really nice place to live too. But did he like it enough to drive an extra ten miles each time he wanted to use a library? Dad repeated that he went there only because he liked the town. Nothing more. He was pretty convincing to me about that.

"What's her name, Simon?"

"Who?"

"Your girlfriend. The one in Hunter."

Dad laughed.

"You were meeting her at the library and then going to her place. We know that. So don't say it's not so. We're beyond that Simon. Who was she?"

Dad just shook his head at them.

"So what was it Simon? Twice a day? Once with Sunny and once with what's her name?"

Sanchez made sure he was on the other side of the table when he made that crack in case Dad blew up again. Good cop Brewer immediately stepped in to say that the barb wasn't fair, and other things too to soothe Dad down.

They wanted a confession, not a fight.

There was no girlfriend. I'm convinced of that. But I also didn't understand why Dad would drive all that way and not just use the computer at home if all he wanted was to go on the Internet. I had to admit that it didn't make sense. Even to me.

Of course I was scared. If Dad couldn't even explain himself, or wouldn't, then what did that mean? I couldn't connect the dots in a straight line or even a zigzagging one. I didn't even have all the dots. Did Dad simply like the town enough to drive the extra miles?

One of the tricks interrogators use is to skip from subject to subject to try to confuse you, so you can't keep track of what you said and maybe you'll be caught in a lie. In the tape, the bad cop detective would sometimes interrupt his own line of questioning by trying to get my Dad's goat, sometimes ridiculing his book or risking saying something more that was insulting to Mom. Then Sanchez and Brewer would join sides, look at each other and talk as if Dad wasn't there, saying things like, "What kind of person needs a book to tell'em how to fuck?" Dad wouldn't bite. Then they ridiculed Dad's use of the term "special culmination," saying Dad wasn't man enough to just use the words that *real men* use. Another ploy to piss him off was having the bad cop look at the other and say, "You know, if my wife looked like Sunny, I'd do it twice a day too." Of course there was a round of laughter from everyone but Dad.

It really pissed me off too.

I've read Dad's book a number of times. He never mentions S & M specifically, which was good, but he does mention how people sometimes have fantasies and urges that can be misunderstood as trying to harm someone. He says that some people need *relief* because of their efforts to try prop up their ego. Dad explains that the ego is really an unending project throughout life, that it has to be built up and defended so the person is assured that they are attractive and capable and all that. Sometimes there's so much worry and pressure, a terrible stress, he emphasized, that people need relief from it, what Dad called a "respite from vulnerability." So they turn to practices that the public doesn't accept.

Okay, maybe that includes S & M. And maybe for some, twice a day can be the substitute relief they need rather than the weird stuff. After the guys were laughing at Dad for using the phrase *special culmination* so much, I too wondered why he kept using the term. He could have just said the usual, or used one of the cruder terms people use for it. But he does use the word "orgasm" a couple of times in his book, so maybe when he used *special culmination* it was a reminder to the reader that it's more special than we think, a kind of healing time, just like he said in his book. "Orgasm" and other words for it are overused and pretty trite, often implying simply "getting off." So maybe Dad used *special culmination* to remind his reader of "getting well."

I'm remembering now how Lily, one of my girlfriends in high school, told me she had sex with this guy via the usual backseat squirms and contortions. She said he finished right away and then had the nerve to ask — *Did you get yours?* Can you imagine? Like there was something to go out and *get*. Of course she hadn't *gotten* anything, but she was too embarrassed to say so. She said, "It was so wonderful, Len. I'll never forget it." I'm sure she wouldn't forget it for a different reason, and I'm sure the guy went away proud. But that was hardly the "special culmination" my Dad talked about, especially since it was a total lie.

Despite Dad being really open about sex when I talked to him last week, he wasn't much of a sex counselor when I was growing up especially when Mom wasn't around to say all the things that could be said girl-to-girl. Once I came home and asked Dad what the ugly 'c' word meant. He was calm and cool and spoke without stuttering as he told me it was an insulting word for a wonderful part of my body and that sometimes guys called girls that to reduce them to just that body part. The whole time Dad's voice was steady, perfectly even, but his face was flushed more than I'd ever seen it.

Dad reminded me all the time that because I look so much like Mom, I had to watch out for boys. Of course he was right. Boys are not your friends, regardless of what they tell you, though there may be an honest one out there somewhere. It's a cliché that *boys only want one thing,* but clichés come from repeated experiences. Girls know that a hookup isn't just a movie or a party. *Ever.* Guys expect it, like sliced pickle on the side. I've realized that "hookup" is precisely the right word because it means there's a hook and there's someone who is going to get hooked.

I'm not a fish.

I'm not saying that I have to fight guys off. I don't usually have to because I've developed a cold stare that I can use when I need to. I've scared off a lot of guys. They know this girl can bite.

Once I went to a movie with this guy from my high school; let's call him James. Dad drove us over to Cobleskill; it was our first date. A quarter of the way through the movie the guy stretches his arm out and settles it around my shoulder. It felt good. A little later he's trying to cup me through my blouse. We hadn't even kissed. My first thought was to bite his fingers. But I didn't. I did what I thought Mom would do. I elbowed him in the face as hard as I could and got up. As I reached the aisle he was bent over cupping his face. Better that than me. Thanks, Mom. An occasional response like that and word gets around real fast.

I think it still does.

16

**The desire to hurt the sexual object
is a perversion of the most common sex life.
-Sigmund Freud**

I'M TRYING TO TELL THIS MY WAY. And I've been trying to avoid saying something because it's so hard. Maybe you already know. They found my mom. It was a connect-the-dots thing.

Because of the Christy Jones stuff and then the missing handcuffs, the police started a full area-search all over again even though it had been so many years later. They searched much farther from our home this time. Mom was a mile away. She was on the property owned by Mr. Whitten who had a real estate office on County Route 23 and a lot of acres on Indian Heights Road, mostly wooded. That's where she was, some of her. Apparently she wasn't even buried. She was just there.

My mom.

The whole thing is bad enough for me in my imagination, so I've never had the nerve to look at the pictures, not even at the trial. If they are worse than what's in my head then I know I couldn't take it. But I've learned some of the details. I've learned that part of her still survived and that hair can last a long time.

Apparently Mom's did. Her long braid. There were bones and some skin left, like leather. Pieces of her jeans too. They said her neck was broken. And they found the other pair of handcuffs. Slightly oval with a dragon-etching and three tight hinges. Same type as the other pairs that were in the blue box. The missing pair. Whoever did this was not even respectful enough to take them off her. When the police found Mom, her arms were still back over her head, as though they had been held there. Like Christy Jones' hands had been held.

Now that they had found Mom and the missing pair from the blue box, I thought for sure Dad would go to jail forever because now nobody would believe that he didn't do it. But then Dad brought in a famous lawyer all the way from the city. Mr. Aireys was a short plump man with a two-inch graying beard that came to a point at the bottom. At first I liked Mr. Aireys. Everyone said he was as sharp a lawyer as they come and that he had won a number of unwinnable cases. He regularly frustrated D.A.s with mistrial after mistrial.

I looked him up on the Internet and found that Mr. Howard Aireys — *Howie* to his friends — was fifty-two and had two grown daughters and an infant son from his third marriage. Besides winning unwinnable cases and frustrating D.A.'s, he was also known for getting mobsters off with light sentences. I didn't like that part. *At all.* I didn't like to think of my dad being defended by a guy who works for crooks. It didn't feel right, and I was sure it wouldn't look right to others that Dr. Simon Taylor's lawyer is in the habit of getting bad criminals off.

In my head I knew that Mr. Aireys had a secret place on the water in Miami with wall-to-wall windows where he invites syndicate bosses for wine and cheese. No, that would be vermicelli or cannelloni. The wine would be Chianti, of course. The mobsters would come to "Howie's" with their D-cup babes whose arms draped around them as they lounge in overstuffed chairs. The way I imagined it, they'd bring a couple of babes for Mr. Aireys too. Two at a time and they'd perform hot sex stuff for him. Of course, they would never speak. They'd be like lamps, like pictures on the wall. Gorgeous but not adorable. They'd move slowly when they moved at all, smiling and ready with a head-back laugh at the right time. In my imagination.

Freud says that imagination is driven by primal and potentially savage desires. All I know is that I don't like mobsters getting off, and I don't like women who sell themselves. I didn't much like Mr. Aireys after I learned about who he was.

But the first thing Mr. Aireys did was really good. He challenged the second search of our home and persuaded a higher-up judge that the lower court judge never should have issued the search warrant in the first place. There simply wasn't enough evidence, he said. The higher-up judge agreed, and the search of our house was declared *unreasonable,* and anything that was found — including the blue box with the two pairs of handcuffs — couldn't be used as evidence against Dr. Simon Taylor. Fruit of the poisonous tree was what they called it.

Score two points for Mr. Aireys. The handcuffs couldn't be used in court. Mr. Aireys also announced that whatever happened to Christy Jones when Dad was living at the commune had no connection to my mom's case. Anyway, nothing could be proven about Christy Jones. Nobody could even bring up Christy Jones's name at the trial. If there was even going to be a trial.

But there was this assistant district attorney — Marjorie Davies — who was like a terrier eyeing the postman's pants. Ms.

Marjorie Davies is African American, medium height with a good figure, a pleasant face, and a super-short Afro bob that makes her head look very round. She still hoped to somehow link Dad to the pair of handcuffs found on Mom. Then they could arrest Dad. So Ms. Davies kept working hard to get the blue box and the oval handcuffs back in as evidence, but through a different door. She had her detectives questioning everyone she could, people in town and in the City who knew Dad, and also people who had been at the commune.

"They can't get the handcuffs in evidence, Simon," Mr. Aireys assured us. "They can't even ask about them, unless you take the stand and that isn't going to happen in my lifetime."

So without Dad bringing up the blue box and what was in it, there was no evidence at all. Zero. Zilch. None.

Mr. Aireys smiled. "We'll be fine," he said. "Don't you worry."

I wanted to believe he was right. I wanted to believe a lot of things.

I don't know how autopsies are performed on someone when there's so little left of them. My mom's hair was rotted, and her neck was broken. They said her wrists were broken too, both of them, probably from trying to club the guy who had bound them tight. They found other bones, but none were broken except ones that might have been gnawed by animals after she'd been abandoned there. There wasn't much left under her fingernails. If there had been at one time, it had washed away. The police couldn't tell if anything else had been done to my mom. They found an abandoned wasp nest on her too. I can't even think about it. They did a toxicology report on Mom's hair, and it showed there had been no drugs or odd chemicals in her system at the time she was left there, nothing unusual at all. I could have told them that.

Still fastened to the bottom of her braid was a barrette that I remembered. Mom was finicky about barrettes, always looking for nice ones. She could rarely find one that she really loved. She wouldn't waste money on one that she only *liked*. She had three or four barrettes, was all. Her favorite one, the one they found on her, the one Dad gave her, was a silver oval with the words *ik ōaṅkār* inscribed in it. That's the one she was wearing. *Ik ōaṅkār* means — "One God."

Dad wasn't into religion, but that didn't bother Mom at all. She told me that whatever people believe there's still one God. He doesn't go away. The Sikh name for God is *Waheguru,* but she said I could call God whatever name I wanted. It's the same God. Also, it was Mom who said prayers with us at night. She knew the "Our Father" and she knew the "Hail Mary" too because Dad was from a Catholic family, and if Mom hadn't known it, it would be one more thing for Grandma Janet, the Saint-in-Waiting, to chide Mom about. The last prayer Mom always said at night was her favorite. It was my favorite too. She called it an *Ardās*, the Sikh word for prayer, and it began *Pritham Bhagautee simar kai Gur Nanak layee dhyaaye.* There was a lot more that I couldn't keep up with, but I always said the first words along with Mom. The words mean: *First think of God, then think of Guru Nanak.* Mom would always close with *ik ōaṅkār*. One God. It didn't matter if I understood all the words, she said; I should listen closely to the sounds. She said that beauty can teach us much more than facts.

I love her. I miss her every hour.

Even though assistant D.A. Marjorie Davies had almost nothing on Dad, that didn't stop the media. Everything about my father was reported and then repeated, whatever anyone said, even a lot of made up things. All along Ms. Davies kept her detectives questioning anyone who might have any information at all. I followed the newspapers, and they were saying that Dad was having an affair back then, though no real evidence of it was revealed. In some letters to the editor at the Albany *Times-Union* people speculated about what might have gone on behind closed doors at the "Twice a Day" doctor's office. Some said that he had to have been an adulterer. More than one letter stated that "nobody but a swinger or free-sexer pervert would write such a book." The newspaper columns gossiped about other things too, that there had to have been whips and masks and ball gags; someone even mentioned cellophane sex. I had to look that up.

They didn't know my dad.

One woman did come forth though. She said that she had sex with Dad one time in 2009, and that he had slapped her around and tried to hold her down and choke her. I didn't believe her. I do know, though, how sex can get out of hand. Not personally, but I've seen people having crazy sex on the Internet. Sometimes it can get pretty weird. If that *did* happen between my father and the woman who came forth, she probably wanted it that way, or, maybe when she later thought back about the experience, she amplified everything in her head. Besides, 2009 was four years after my mom was gone; if Dad had waited that long to have sex he was the best man on earth. Still, I couldn't believe that my dad had gone with someone, even for a night. He was always so focused on Mom.

The woman's name was Karen Booth, and she told the newspapers that she had met Dad at The Congress of the Mental Health Association conference in Miami. Dad's famous *Twice- a-Day* book had been out for years, and now he had a lot of articles published too, so he was still in demand. His afternoon address at that conference was on Freud versus Jung and Adler specifically on the question of whether sex was the basis for most motivation. Jung said no, it wasn't. Adler said no, too. Freud said, yes. Two against one, but still.

There were pictures of Karen Booth in the *Post*. She was pretty enough, and pretty young too, maybe around twenty-eight, which means she would have been about twenty-four at the time she claimed to be with my dad. That's too young for her to have been a doctor or psychologist herself, so she could've been at the conference as a meeting planner, a hotel employee, or as a guest at the hotel. The article didn't say. Or maybe she was a sad hanger-on, a wacko who needed help and snuck into the conference for that. Dad could spot those types right off, so I don't think he'd ever have gotten involved with one.

I never asked Dad if he had slept with her, and he never said. At home we didn't talk about gossip or anything that anyone claimed which might be misunderstood. Mom had been gone for so long by then that if there had been an affair, it was hardly "extramarital." If anything, he and Karen Booth just had an amorous time, maybe a little spicy, though the papers made it sound weird and kinky. Dad and Mr. Aireys never discussed her in front of me, but nobody at the newspapers bothered to investigate *her* background. None of it mattered though because Karen Booth couldn't testify to knowing anything about Christy Jones or Mom. Score another point for Mr. Aireys. Still, the Karen Booth story was out there in the papers for everyone to see. Even jury members, if Dad's case went to a jury, and Mr. Aireys still promised that it wouldn't.

Something else that Karen Booth said didn't add up. She said my dad had been drinking a lot. I've never seen him drink anything more serious than a small Scotch whiskey and water, so I doubted what she said about that too. But I know things can happen out of town. Dad may have been needier than I realized. And he's a guy. I couldn't forget that. Dad had always warned me about guys.

On August 14, 2014, the phone rang and I answered it. The woman on the other end was very upset, almost crying. She said her name was Anita Rodgers, which rang a bell, and that she needed to speak to my dad right away.

Mr. Aireys was there then, with his two assistants, Rachel and Elena, who wore pretty much the same glasses and had the same serious faces though they could never have been taken for twins; Rachel was kind of heavy with frizzed up ginger-colored hair, pretty low on the hotness scale; and the taller one, Elena, was pretty but geeky-looking with dark bangs that slanted across her forehead, sometimes hiding her eyes. The frizzed Rachel was mostly in bright colors and the geeky one always in gray. Anyway, we all watched as my dad spoke for some time on the phone, watched him growing more and more tense and grim. Finally he shrugged, shook his head and hung up, then came back to the table and shrugged again, like it was all over.

I knew.

Mr. Aireys knew too.

"Well, well," Mr. Aireys said, even before Dad had explained. His eyes were excited now like he was welcoming a good fight. He leaned forward in his kitchen chair, elbows on the table and steepling his fingers as he stroked the tip of his beard.

"Well, well," he repeated. "Now it's going to get interesting."

Mr. Aireys and his assistants immediately drove over to Anita's house in Richmondville. Dad and I didn't go. Dad wouldn't talk about it anymore with me, but the next day it was reported over and over again on every news channel. Someone had leaked that Anita Rodgers was Dad's former secretary. She told the detectives that she'd come to the office one morning and had seen the blue box and handcuffs. She described them, and they were exactly like those found on Mom. She said that they looked like nickel or maybe shiny stainless steel, and that they had triple hinges rather than the usual links between the cuffs. Instead of being round, they were a bit oval and they had markings on each side, like a dragon or a serpent.

Now if there was a Grand Jury, and Anita Rogers was brought to the stand, the D.A. would hold up the handcuffs that were found on Mom and ask, "Are these the same kind that you saw at Dr. Taylor's office?" She would have to say, "Yes." Then the handcuffs would be in, the worst evidence against Dad. There would be a trial after all, and of course that would be horrible.

Anita also told the prosecutor's office that the handcuffs were on top of some books on Dad's desk. They were next to the blue box. He wasn't trying to hide them at all, she said. When she came in to work that day she noticed them and jokingly said something like, "Looks like one of your patients came prepared."

Dad had laughed, and answered, "Everybody needs something, Anita."

So Dad hadn't told the truth about the handcuffs. They *were* his. But at least he hadn't been trying to hide them, so maybe that means something. They were right there on his desk. He was even casual enough about them and had innocently enough said — *Everybody needs something, Anita.* Maybe that's true, and maybe he was just saying it because it's true. That didn't make him a murderer.

Later that day Mr. Aireys came back with his two assistants and we sat at the kitchen table again.

"You know, Simon, it will get even worse if the D.A. gets hold of your credit card statements and finds a purchase in your name from the company that sold them." He looked at Dad and I looked at Dad. We all waited. Dad was looking out the window. "I won't be able to object to the credit card statements as evidence," Mr. Aireys went on. "There's nothing I can do about that."

Dad was still looking out the window.

The more I thought about Dad not telling the truth and the possibility of a trial, the more scared I got. I started to get angry about what everyone was thinking about Dad. I told myself there was no *real* proof that he had done anything to Mom; but I knew the handcuffs could be enough to convict him if jury members connected the handcuffs to all the blather about him in the papers and on TV.

Did Dad do it? He had lied about the handcuffs, even to me. But I still wasn't convinced. *Everybody needs something, Anita.*

Maybe so, but even that couldn't persuade me.

17

**In the depths of my heart I can't help
being convinced that my dear fellow-men—
with a few exceptions—are worthless.
-Sigmund Freud**

MY MOM HAD A FAVORITE SAYING: "Wishes are stones that do not float." She would say that whenever I told her school was too easy and I wished I could stay home and just read, or that I wished I could grow up faster. Mom had others too, but she wouldn't say them like some old grandmother snapping them off over her shoulder. They were *truths*. When she said them she would always stop and hold me against her or look at me intensely. "Annie, if you want to have a fragrance, then you have to be a flower." Or, when I wanted to read and watch cartoons at the same time, she'd say, "Oh my dear Annie. *Waheguru* wants you to do *something*, not everything."

When I spoke to Dad last week, he reminded me of another one: "Hands to work, heart to God." That was Mom all the time.

After the handcuffs were in, that's when I got busy collecting my own evidence. If we were going to trial, maybe I could be the one who solved the case. I went through the old police records and watched the interviews and TV shows like *Dateline* that I hadn't seen. Not just to help Dad find out what really happened, though. I also wanted to understand my parents.

What kept popping into my mind was what Dad said to a lot of his patients: *Inside every person is another person deprived of what he really wants.* If Dad was right, everyone has this other self who is hidden inside—the judge did, Ms. Davies, Grandpa and even Grandma Janet the Saint-in-Waiting. All of us. Veronica, too, I suppose, who was already throwing out her frayed tomboy shorts and trying to talk Dad into letting her wear halter tops. Maybe that "inside person" is there even for me. Maybe it gets loose at a certain age. Maybe that person is dark and even scary, and grows slowly but when she's fully developed she breaks out and makes the outer person do things she'd never dream of doing before.

Freud talked a lot about the *id*, and maybe that's what Dad was referring to as "the person inside us." *Id* is Latin for "it." Freud calls it our basic unorganized urges, sudden impulses that don't make judgments and can't tell good from evil. Maybe Freud called it the *id*, the it, because it's so unconscious that there's nothing there that we can really point to. It's just *there*. Like the air around us. Like the thoughts the flutter through of their own accord. Freud wanted his patients to know this "other person"—their inner hypocrite and cheat and liar who knows no morality. He wanted this "other person" to surface and walk around and feel the breeze and the disinfecting sunlight. Hopefully his patients would then get better.

Okay, I had to admit that Dad must also feel this other person inside him who is deprived of his deepest desires, or else Dad wouldn't know so much about it and focus on it so much. Freud even says that it's good for a therapist to have his own neurosis.

Then he can empathize with others more fully. I guess a shrink with no problems is like a dentist who's never had a cavity drilled. He can't understand.

But there's one thing I don't agree with Freud about — that people are pretty much worthless. Mom wasn't worthless. I can't remember her doing anything wrong. Even the times she was arrested she hadn't done anything she thought was immoral. She was filled with love all the time; she was always doing good things. She always told me that the purpose of life is to love God and love the truth. "Truth is all that matters, Annie. Whatever it is." So maybe Freud was wrong. I'm not sure yet, but if Freud was wrong about that, then Dad was wrong about a lot of things too. It's confusing. But it doesn't mean Dad did anything to his wife, Sunny, or to that girl Christy Jones.

I've also thought about Dad's mirror phobia, and what mirrors mean psychologically, symbolically. Could his mirror phobia have something to do with this person inside him? A broken mirror is supposed to mean bad luck. But Dad was never superstitious. He and Mom believed in hard work, not luck. In our home, mirrors weren't hung on the walls, as I said. We had to be very careful. Dad used to joke about his *thing* sometimes, but Mom never did. She treated it seriously in front of us, and of course none of us ever spoke about it to anyone outside the house. It was *family business.* We didn't even talk about it to Grandpa Sam and Grandma Janet, though maybe they knew about it from when Dad was a boy. I didn't know when his phobia started. It wasn't like he had a brain tumor or a bursting appendix. He was just *Dad,* and the mirror thing was part of him. *Everybody needs something, Anita.* I guess everybody has something they are dealing with.

When I free-associate about mirrors I come up with this list:

- ✓ Broken mirror — superstitious people say it's bad luck.
- ✓ Mirrors are a symbol for reflection — what a therapist is supposed to be good at.
- ✓ When I look in a mirror, someone is watching me. It's me.
- ✓ A mirror reverses everything, even if I don't notice it.
- ✓ Mirrors only reflect things when there's enough light.
- ✓ Mirrors can distort things, making them look bigger or smaller or funny.
- ✓ Narcissus, the myth: He looks in the water and falls in love with his own reflection.

I read about narcissism in Freud, but Dad is definitely not narcissistic. Freud says that narcissistic behavior is part of the normal human condition when we're very young, and that later it regresses if the person becomes a healthy adolescent or adult. Another idea I had is way out there, but I had to face it: Maybe Dad did do something wrong, and now he can't look at himself in the mirror. Christy Jones had been strangled in the water while she was being drowned. Water . . . mirror.

I force myself to imagine someone drowning Christy, someone who is jealous or angry and who pushes his beloved's head in the water, his hands tight around her throat as he sees her thrashing and hears the helpless gulps, all the bubbles rising to the surface and bursting in front of him; and when she is silent, the water becomes still and smooth again, and the person leans over Christy in the pond, like Narcissus did, and sees himself in the smooth reflection; except he doesn't understand what happened, or how. And instead of falling in love with himself, as

Narcissus had, now the man hates himself. He wants to flee. But others in the community are already running toward him, so he pretends that he found the girl already dead. Someone else did it.

Like I said, that theory is way out there. The more I think about maybe being a therapist, the more difficult and demanding I realize the profession is. I still have so much to learn about everything. But if I keep going, I'll get there.

And I have to get there.

PART II

18

The tendency to inflict and receive pain during sexual intercourse are the most common and important of all perversions.
-Sigmund Freud

More Things That People Said

I'll bet Sunny just went along with it. It was all his doing.
— Tod Nettles[18]

I *don't know what Simon had bottled up in there. But I'll bet it wasn't nice.* — Tina Simmons[19]

In my experience a lot of times the ones who seem really nice are hiding something. They know they're split between good and evil, idealizing and demonizing others, and afraid they'll end up humiliating or even hurting those around them. I think Sunny probably pushed him somehow, and he just went off. It wasn't necessarily sexual. — James Henry, Psychiatric Nurse, WMSS Division, Connecticut Valley Hospital

---

[18] Roger Nettles, neighbor, interviewed by the *Post* reporter Francis Hackman. July 19, 2014.
[19] Tina Simmons, neighbor, interviewed by the *Post* reporter Francis Hackman. July 19, 2014.

Neither the Church nor the Bible explicitly consider sadism as a taboo or even a sin. —Father Roger Donahue, Diocese of Rockville Centre, Long Island, New York[20]

It's been years since I went to him. I was going through a difficult time in my life; I still think about Dr. Taylor and how he helped me. He was filled with such kindness and compassion. He helped me get out from under my cloud and into the sunshine again. I think everyone who knew him also cared so much about him. —Sandra Epps[22]

Simon said there was no such thing as a perversion. That's what he told me. —Name withheld[21]

---

[20] *New York Times.* Interview, October 21, 2014.
[21] Former patient. Name withheld upon request.
[22] Former patient. *New York Times* interview. October 24, 2014.

19

**We have long observed that every neurosis
has the result of forcing the patient out of real
life, of alienating him from actuality.
-Sigmund Freud**

THEY CAME FOR MY DAD ON A WEDNESDAY MORNING. TWO cars. Rainbow started growling and pawing the door with his only front paw. I had to put him in the basement. I knew right away what was happening.

They knocked loudly; I went to the door and told them Dad wasn't home. But his car was in the driveway so they knew he was. They pushed past me and found my dad in the back study. They turned him around and cuffed him. They led him away. Veronica didn't see, but I did. Now it's just Veronica and Rainbow and me.

Later they booked him and took his photograph from the front and side while he held a little sign with his numbers on it. Dad would go before a judge the next day and the judge would ask, "How do you plead?" Dad or Mr. Aireys would say, "Not guilty, Your Honor." Dad's lawyer would argue about bail with the prosecutor, Ms. Marjorie Davies. She would say that Simon Taylor is a man of means and therefore a flight risk. *Your Honor, just look at the heinous nature of the crime.* Mr. Aireys would counter that Dr. Taylor is a professional and an upstanding citizen with a long history in this state; he's the father of two children—one who is a minor. But bail would be set high because my dad had resources.

It was set at two million, which I thought Dad would have for sure, but it turned out that he couldn't pay it *and* pay Mr. Airey's half million, which was what he wanted for starters. So our house was used for collateral. Dad had to ask my grandparents to put up theirs as well.

The bond company was *Bernardo's Bail Bonds* in Albany. I never saw Bernardo but I'm sure he was fat with real strong arms and smoked heavily and sat behind a small desk in his office with a stony stare that said he was half pissed off at everything in the world and that the other half of him was just bored to death. He had seen it all, so he could give everyone the hairy eyeball when they came to him for help. He was their savior.

Everyone is a shrink these days, even me, I guess. So gossip hounds analyzed what they knew or thought they knew about Dad. Anyone could do the math. But it didn't add up to "beyond a reasonable doubt" to me, so I didn't see how it could for all twelve jurors. No way.

If anyone knew about my dad's mirror phobia they might factor that in too, even though it's irrelevant. But no one knew about it outside our family. His attorney sure didn't. So the issue wouldn't come up at trial. Even if it were somehow brought up, it wouldn't be relevant. A nonfactor, as they say. But if it got on TV, then Dad would seem even weirder than everyone already thought.

Let them all try to be shrinks if that makes them happy. I think I'm a little more qualified to look at the facts and understand them because I've been around psychiatry all my life. And I've been around my dad.

Freud said that if an inner conflict ends only in a neurosis, then it can be quite harmless, and maybe even be a "socially tolerable" solution to the problem. He's obviously *not* saying that there's anything socially tolerable about what happened to Mom. About being a psychoanalyst, I read where Freud said that if you give it your finger, it will take your whole hand. I think that's what Dad meant when he said things can stick to you. I can feel that every time I think about the case. To be an analyst takes patience and tireless examination. That's how I wanted to approach my dad's situation. The trouble is that he's my dad. When I thought that he and Mom may have been a little different in the privacy of their bedroom than I had thought, I tried hard to remember that they were still wonderful parents and both of them made great contributions to society. The handcuffs didn't mean they were into S & M. That would be too much. The reports about whips and ball gags — I had to believe it was all media gossip. They didn't have facts. They just wanted titillating news. Yes, I know that Dad is pretty liberal about a lot of things. Still, my mom couldn't be in on it. Me and the rest of the country analyzing them wouldn't help at all. Nothing got clearer. Even today it's not much clearer.

I have a friend at college who's a little older than I am. She's mostly Asian, has long hair and a long body. Her name is Connie; she's twenty-three and a senior. We've gone to some movies, watched TV together in her room, and just sort of hung out sometimes. If I can use one of Freud's words, Connie is definitely more *libidinous* than I am. She was in my dorm room here at Union; we were sitting cross-legged on my bed, talking. This was before the trial started but everyone at school seemed to know about the blue box and what was in it, and about the false gossipy things too. I was embarrassed. I think that Connie was trying to assure me that normal people sometimes like doing things that aren't so normal.

Connie said that she liked to be blindfolded. Sometimes. And restrained. Just a little, she said. Not all the time, but enough of the time. She said it made her feel vulnerable, yet somehow safe too. She wasn't stupid, she told me, and she knew the guy she did it with real well—Brad. They were going to be married after she graduated. She said that she had made the blindfold herself by cutting it out from some heavy cloth in a way that it could cover her eyes and then taper in the back so it could be easily tied. She said she made a little play of it whenever she got the blindfold out. Brad would put it on her, reaching around to tie it. He would tie her hands in front of her too, with a scarf she had. Then she would lay back and relax, she said, and withdraw into herself just allowing herself to be a bundle of senses as they did whatever they did.

I think she was waiting for me to share one of my experiences about doing it in a special way that I preferred. I didn't want to tell her that I hadn't had any complete experiences, just lots of touching everywhere, and that was enough for now. I thought about making up a halfway hot story for her benefit, but it would have been a lie. I wanted to have her as a close friend so I needed to be truthful; even if I did try to come up with something to tell her, it probably would have seemed pretty tame compared to her love-making, like I know hers is pretty tame compared to a lot of others. So I didn't say anything at all.

Freud explains it this way: He says that we have sexual urges even as infants, but that our urges don't yet have any direction.

He says they're still ambiguous when we're young, but in time they could go this way or that way, and that because of people's experiences, some become attached to breasts rather than feet, leather over silk, cross-dressing over whatever. I've read about dacryphila, which is when you get turned on by someone crying. There's even something called plushophilia, which is being aroused by the sight of a teddy bear. Go figure. Freud says that our urges find their direction as we grow up; it becomes part of our personal sexual makeup. It's not really a perversion, he claims, except when people compare it to what they consider to be "normal." I think he meant that what we tell each other is normal is probably not what many are really doing in private.

Maybe my early childhood was real boring because I don't feel drawn to anything much except what some people call "vanilla." I've seen all the ways they do it on the Internet, all of them, but it's still hard for me to understand handcuffs. I even found a site *Whips & Chains* where they talked about etiquette at their *parties*: Keep an open mind. Moderate alcohol. Be polite. If someone has a collar on, that means they are *owned*, so don't approach them for *play*. Dress in your favorite fetish costume, if you have one—nun, nurse, teacher. Or dress sexy at least. If someone is role-playing a punishment scene, and it bothers you, don't look. Be discreet—you may recognize people there who you thought led vanilla lives. Respect their privacy and confidentiality.

I try to be honest with myself; Freud says that being entirely honest with oneself is a good exercise. But I just don't get S & M. I don't get trig or statistics either, so it could just be me.

After Dad was out on bail, he let me sit in and listen whenever Mr. Aireys was at the house talking about the case. Dad wanted me to be part of what was going on. He wanted me to learn everything I could, but he wanted me to learn it directly from them, not from TV or the press. One time Grandpa Sam and Grandma Janet happened to be over, but Dad wouldn't include them. Just me. It felt good. I saw Grandma Janet's dirty look as she left the den and closed the door on her way out, as Dad had requested.

Sometimes Dad and Mr. Aireys would argue about something and I would get up and head to the kitchen and feed Rainbow or rearrange the refrigerator shelves or pretend to do some dishes, the water running very slowly so I could hear. Whenever voices were really raised I knew it was because Dad was telling his lawyer that he wanted to take the stand. Mr. Aireys wouldn't hear of it. Mr. Aireys always said that *he* knew what taking the stand meant, and *Dad* didn't. I remember one time Mr. Aireys slowing down his speech and saying, "Simon, it-means-they-will-tear-you-apart-up-there. You-just-can't-see-how-dangerous-it-is. You can be as righteous and stubborn as you want—after it's over. Until then you say nothing, nothing-at-all. Do you understand? I'm the one who does the thinking and the talking, do you hear? Do you hear me, Simon?"

No answer from my dad; I knew he was staring coldly at Mr. Aireys.

"Damn it, Simon, I know what I'm doing. If you don't trust me, then get someone else."

The whole house would be silent around Mr. Aireys' threat, except for the trickle of water from the faucet in front of me. My ear was focused on the conversation coming from the next room, but nothing more was said. Even Rainbow didn't stir. Silence is a strange thing. It can absorb into the couch and chairs and lay itself flat on the old hardwood floors. Just the trickle of water, and beyond it the silence, but I knew Dad was holding back a scream.

After Mr. Aireys left that day, I did a major clean up in the kitchen. Everything wiped dry and put away, even the top of the refrigerator got wiped clean. I was leaving my dad alone to sit in the living room and think. Finally I told him I was going to bed. I kissed him on his forehead five times, counting as I went. He cracked a smile and said, "Good night, Annie. Sleep well."

My room hasn't been painted since high school, so I still have the dark green and blue walls with my white handwriting on them, lines from some songs, like:

The lights go out and I can't be saved,
Tides I tried to swim against,

It's from Coldplay. I didn't even like them anymore.

I didn't get changed for bed right away, just lay there on top of the covers thinking, my school books on the floor. I hadn't touched them for some time, and had only gone to a few of my classes. There were some magazines on the bed that I had picked up when Dad and I stopped at the market that afternoon. Not any of the scandal sheets near the checkout stand that reported which celebrity is having whose baby and which aging actress is dying of some strange disease. I'd pulled out *Glamour* and *Self* from the other rack. At the checkout, I looked up at Dad to make sure it was okay if we bought them. "Of course, baby," he said.

When Dad knocked on my door a little later, I had the *Glamour* magazine open and was turning pages, though I hardly saw even the pictures. Inside the magazine Rihanna was answering her fans' questions; there were revelations from those who knew the best nail tips, and even a page on how giving oral sex is empowering. Great. Dad came in and sat on the edge of the bed.

"Anything good in there?"

"Lots," I said. "If you need an instant tan or a perky push-up bra."

"What about a horoscope," he asked. "What's it say for this month?"

Dad is a Pisces, so I found the horoscope section and read it. It was about making yourself available to a pal even if you have to reschedule a casual social plan.

"Sounds as pertinent as a penguin on Pluto," Dad said. That was an expression he'd come up with every once in a while. He asked what my horoscope was. I'm a Libra. I'm balanced. That's me. My horoscope said I was being too objective in my life and I needed to bring my emotions forward. Thanks a lot.

"Should we look up Mr. Aireys?" I asked.

"I'm sure he's not an Aries. He's got to be a Taurus."

I looked up Taurus, and it fit Mr. Aireys to a T. It said that his profile is high and now is a great time for self-promotion. Momentum is building.

"Anything good in there about sex?" Dad asked then.

"Dad."

"Just wondering."

"No, Dad."

"We don't talk about sex, and I don't know anything that's going on with you, sweetheart."

I rolled the magazine into a tube.

"Girls talk to their moms," he went on.

"Or to other girls."

"Great. The blind leading the blind."

"Not always so blind. Besides, everything's fine." I knew he didn't really want to talk about sex either.

"Well, you let me know, will you? I haven't been much of a parent lately. I know you've been going through a lot. I'm not as cool as your mom would have been." Dad gave me his *Dad* look. "You watch out for boys."

"I know. I know."

"Okay, I'm going to ask." He paused as if having a hard time getting it out, and then finally said, "Are you having sex?"

"Dad, please."

"Baby, it's not like smoking pot."

"Can we change the subject?"

"I don't even know if you're going out with boys at college now, Annie."

"I think boys are scared of me."

"I never would have asked your mom out either, you know that? She was too beautiful."

"Veronica is going to be beautiful too."

"I know."

"Dad, what was it like to be married to someone so beautiful?"

He smiled, and I knew he was remembering something. "I'd see the looks your mom got on the street," he said, "from everyone: middle-aged men and younger men, even teenagers and old men. A lot of the time from women too."

"We're defensive, Dad. We're always checking out the competition."

"Even your grandparents," Dad added.

"Really?"

"You know, your grandpa has always been a lady's man. Your mom and I would joke about it, how your grandmother would have to keep an eye on your grandfather when he visited us because Grandpa Sam kept an eye on your mom." Dad laughed. "Your mom said she was certain his interest was . . . what did she call it? Oh, yes, your mom called it your grandpa's *aesthetic appreciation*. I never appreciated it though. But you already know that my dad and I have a bit of a difficult relationship."

"Yuck. How could Grandpa Sam act that way?"

"He's a guy, baby. Besides, everyone looked at your mom. And thoughts aren't actions, baby. Actions are the only things that count. Anyway, your grandparents loved Sunny because she made me so happy and because she and I made you and your sister."

He was quiet a moment. "Now, tell me about school, sweetheart? I haven't seen you doing any homework."

"Like I can. I may have to drop out and start over again next semester. I don't really mind."

"That's fine. It's an important time for your mother too, not just me. Let's do it right so there's no regrets."

"Got it. Thanks, Dad." He kissed me on my forehead five times, counting. He left in a wandering kind of way. I knew he was thinking about the trial, and like me, he was afraid of what could happen.

20

Where there is love, there is no sin.
-Sigmund Freud

MR. AIREYS WAS EVEN AGAINST ME BEING AT COURT. He thought I might be disruptive or a distraction to Dad. He said that Dad needed to look poised and professional every time the jury glanced over at him, not worrying about what his daughter was thinking all the time.

I told Mr. Aireys that was okay for Veronica — she was only twelve — but that I was eighteen, not a minor, and I'd be there for moral support. Besides, there was no legal way he could keep me out. I'd get there on my own if I had to. I'd even hitch-hike. Or walk all the way. Or run. I was going to be there for my dad.

Dad said he was afraid it might scar me, seeing the photos of my mom, what was left of her. I didn't care. I wouldn't look. I'd walk around the block. Even if I did see the photos, they would be nothing like hearing about it on the news and seeing my dad go to jail without me being there to help in some way.

After a silent standoff between us, Mr. Aireys nodded to my dad.

"It'll work, Simon. A trial is only part evidence. The rest is illusion, and a lot of theater . . . "

"Illusion! And theater? Dad's life . . . "

Mr. Aireys held up his hand to stall me. "The point is that it'll work if she's there," he said, still talking only to Dad. "It'll make you seem more like a neighbor or one of the parents at their kid's ball game."

He was right, but it wasn't illusion or theater. *Dr. Taylor has a daughter who stands by him despite what he's accused of. The shrink couldn't be a psycho then. He couldn't have done it if his kid still loves him.* It would be good, because every juror will have seen movies of slashers in hockey masks who were loners living on the outskirts of town somewhere and thought nobody understood them. Or TV shows about guys who traveled the interstates looking for women. They weren't established professionals like my dad with nice-looking children.

Finally my dad nodded too. I would be an asset after all. I had convinced them both.

I knew that the jury pool might have some people who already hated Dr. Simon Taylor without even knowing him. Some of them could be husbands who thought that if they set my dad free he might do to their wives what he'd done to Sunny. Or maybe some jurors were even afraid *they* were capable of something like that. Or one of the possible jurors was the real one who took Mom. Some jurors might be women who had learned to hate men because they were forced into S & M by their husbands. I hoped that some might have read his great book. Then they'd know what he was like. Just one jury member, and it'd be a hung jury that Mr. Aireys was famous for. That's all it would take, just one. Just one.

When Mom and Dad met at that restaurant in the City, she said she could *feel* him. She could *feel* who he was. I don't think dad *feels* people and the world the way my mom did. He lives a lot more upstairs in his head just like most guys. He sorts out things by thinking hard or by going through a lot of books. But somehow Dad knew right away that Mom was the one for him. He trusted Mom. Everybody trusted her. She was clear and honest and mostly direct. Dad could see right away that if Sunny loved you, she'd love you forever.

I guess I'm trying to analyze them here even if I know it's only a half-educated analysis. I also know that when Mom was around I didn't know hardly any of the things that I know now. She was just there, being my warm Mom, and like every young kid I didn't know to look at her as a psychological and spiritual being, or to try to understand her. She was supposed to understand *me*. What I realize now is that the inner part of Mom shone through all the time. I also know that there's an inner part of people that has needs that are so private, maybe even dark and scary, and so guarded that they almost never let it out. That's what marriage is for. Trust and intimacy. If Mom and Dad used fluffy pink handcuffs with break-away Velcro or the real hard kind that clink shut tight, I don't care. Maybe there was a lot more that they did together. I still don't care.

I was surprised how casually the jury pool arrived at court the first day of the trial, like it was a ball game and they didn't know how important it was. The judge even had to tell one of them to take his sunglasses off. My dad wore a nice suit and he was able to go home at night because he had posted the huge bond with the help of Grandma Janet, the Saint-in-Waiting and Grandpa

Sam, the Bicycle and Ladies' Man. They even moved in with us for a time to look after Veronica and Rainbow when I went with Dad to court each day. I always sat right behind him. I was right there for him, and always will be.

Mr. Aireys had his two female assistants sitting to his right. They dressed conservatively, and they both wore their glasses. The plan was that throughout the trial they would smile at my dad whenever they spoke to him. Message to the jury: *Smart, young women aren't afraid of Dr. Simon Taylor, so no one else should be either.* The jury members would see those smiles more than once.

I liked the judge because he had thrown out the blue box and the handcuffs they'd found in our house. But that's all I liked about him. His name was Judge Wickersham, and he might have been a pretty good judge but he was what my dad used to call a "grump face" when I was growing up. "Don't be a grump-face, Annie," Dad would scold when I was in a sour mood. "Veronica, you're going to be stuck with that grump face all your life if you don't change it right now." He would usually do something silly then to make us laugh, like go in the corner and try to stand on his head. He never could quite do it though; he always ended up falling over. Sometimes he'd just say, "Don't be such a grump face," and he'd start heading to the corner — and that's all it took. We'd be laughing hard.

Judge Wickersham had crisscross lines on his forehead, and his grump face made me think from the start that he didn't like my dad. Maybe it was because he'd already formed an opinion about Simon Taylor or maybe it was because the judge had tried *Twice a Day* with his wife and it hadn't worked. Just a thought.

The judge cautioned the jury not to watch the news or read anything about the case after they left the courtroom. All the evidence would be presented in court or it wasn't true evidence. He was really stern about that, which was great because you couldn't walk down the street in Albany and not see the headlines on the corner stand: *"Twice a Day Starts Today"* and *"Twice a Day, Maybe for Life."* The tabloids were worse: *"Twice a Day Doc Kills Twice."*

Christy Jones's parents were at the courthouse too. That first morning they stood on the sidewalk holding up a big picture of their daughter with a sign that said, *Help Our Christy Rest.* Because of the papers and TV reporting, everyone knew what the sign meant. But there was no proof about anything that happened back then at the commune, except that my dad had once lived there — along with a bunch of other guys — and that he had been the one who found Christy's body.

The picture that Christy's parents held up was obviously from before she turned hippie. It was a black-and-white, probably a blowup from her high school yearbook. Christy looked as pretty as ever in a dark sweater with hair that fell softly on her shoulders. She wore a simple white necklace, and her head was slightly tilted as she smiled winningly at the camera.

Christy's parents were on the news a lot but I never watched. The TV was hardly on now in our home. Inside the courtroom, Christy's parents looked old and angry and tired. They had never given up, and they believed that "getting justice" was somehow going to help them put everything behind them. Right.

Oh, and that reporter was there too, Will Halverton. He was a classically rumpled newspaperman with narrow, rectangular glasses and a constantly sneering smile. He sat on the other side of the room from me, watching everything and reporting it later that day. I hated him.

Fifty-five potential jurors were brought in that first morning. Twelve would be chosen and some alternates. Mr. Aireys had told us the week before that the judge would probably bring in more than the usual twenty or so because he expected a number of exclusions. Even more jurors from the pool were waiting in the jury lounge in case Mr. Aireys and Ms. Davies still couldn't find twelve.

From the start, Ms. Marjorie Davies was all competence. Formal and erect, she looked like the consummate professional who knew the facts and knew beforehand what the result should be. She scared me. Mr. Aireys had told Dad and me that women and blacks generally gained sympathy among most people, especially when opposing a white man.

Before the lawyers began their round of questioning, each side already knew the names and some facts about each juror from the jury questionnaire that Mr. Aireys and Ms. Davies had agreed on. Based on the jurors' answers, they and their staffs had then combed public records, Facebook, and other social media websites to find out anything they could about who would be deciding if my father was guilty of murdering Sunny Taylor.

Mr. Aireys said that that jury selection was probably the most important part of a trial. "There's both fate and luck here," he said. "You ask the right question to the right jury to get the answer you really need." He even had an investigators drive by their homes to check out their cars and toys in their garages, even slogans on bumper stickers.

"Size and type of your home, and type of car," he had said, "can say a lot. All American-made? Then likely they are 'belongers.' Nationalistic. They don't like change. We find a flashy car with a young, apparently financially insecure person, then he's trying to look big. A minivan? They're typically calm people and they aren't loners. Beat up pickups used for work means they're full time workers, probably service-related jobs, middle income to poor. Rust bucket of a truck? It's paid off, and he's broke or not status conscious. A Honda says they're practical. BMW says they make 125K or more. The best indicator," he went on, "is often the bumper stickers. Stick-figure parents and kids on the rear window. *No Nukes. NRA. Tea Party.*

He took a breath and looked directly at Dad. "I've won cases on bumper stickers alone, Simon. That, and I want to look the person in the eye. See how they answer a question; quickly, hesitantly, eyes flashing away. I've got a good sense. Trust me."

Mr. Aireys and Ms. Davies each had a limited number of exclusions based only on the facts they'd dug up so far, and their questions and intuition. Mr. Aireys had told us that if he didn't like someone's profession or marital status or something in his or her history, he would try to find a way to exclude them *for cause.* Jurors who had police officers in their families were to be immediately excluded as well as those who lost a family member through violence. Mr. Aireys wouldn't take chances on that. Would men be more sympathetic to my dad or to woman? Did we want smart people or dumb? Professionals or Joe down the street? Did the juror look like a Mormon? If so, that might work in my dad's favor because of Mormons' supposed views on women. Could one juror secretly be a biker? That would be in my dad's favor too. The final twelve and five alternates would be determining the outcome of Dad's life. Mr. Aireys had to get it right.

When the questioning started, Mr. Aireys did not ask anyone *if* he or she went to church, but *where* they went to church. I guess that was supposed to get more at the truth.

Have you ever been arrested? Not even a DUI?

Do you own a gun?

Tell me a little about your neighborhood.

On her turns, Ms. Davies went from person to person with confidence, as though she somehow knew the perfect questions to ask.

What TV shows do you watch?

How many times have you been married?

Do you have children? Oh, how many? How old?

Is any member of your family taking antidepressants or antipsychotic medicine?

After each answer she would nod at the person, and keep nodding, which was her way of keeping them talking so she could learn even more.

If you could eliminate one crime from the world, what would it be?

Do you ever blog? Oh, about what? How interesting!

Ms. Davies was crisp, friendly, and personal. Her wide smile showed her perfect white teeth. I could see why she would be arguing the case for the state. I didn't like her.

Mr. Aireys was a bit too formal for my liking. Not a lot, just a little. He seemed too dressed up, compared with the jurors anyway. Would they be able to identify with him? I wondered. If they wouldn't be able to identify with Mr. Aireys then they wouldn't identify with my dad. I learned that the old saying is, *While the lawyers are picking a jury, the jury is picking the lawyers.* Candor, integrity, competence.

I'm sure most of the jurors recognized Mr. Aireys' famous face and beard, but to me he seemed full of himself. His smile didn't work on them like Ms. Davies' smile. He just wasn't like-able. I was afraid that Dad had made a thousand dollar an hour mistake.

Have you ever been falsely accused of anything? Can you share how you felt?

Can you return a verdict based on the clear facts and not on a TV show hunch?

Have you ever seen someone handcuffed in real life? On TV? What did you think?

Do you think you'll know an innocent person when the facts show that?

Mr. Aireys was telling them right off that Dad was innocent, and asking if they would be able to see that he was? Still, Mr. Aireys came across as pompous. Where Ms. Davis walked with sure purpose, he sometimes seemed to strut. He was a game show host. He was a movie celebrity. I kept thinking that if he couldn't even win me over, how could he win the jury over? Dad didn't seem to notice, though. I had to stop my thoughts from the crazed maze they were falling in. Mr. Aireys was the pro. He got real murderers off. He got mafia leaders six months. Then I'd find myself obsessing again about how he wasn't the right lawyer for my dad, which made me want to slap my leg and laugh loudly.

Do you agree that people from small towns are better at keeping open minds?

He was trying to butter them up, but I didn't believe they were buying it. I wanted to trust him, but even more I wanted to climb into my dad's lap and cry.

It went on all morning and continued after lunch and then through the rest of the afternoon. The next day too, and part of

Wednesday. Some were excused for this or that, or because of something Ms. Davies and Mr. Aireys had found in their background, or something they couldn't quite pinpoint.

Mr. Aireys had already explained to us that his goal was to put as many different kinds of people as possible on the jury. Not just butchers and bakers and candlestick makers, he said, because they were all tradesmen. He said we needed a black person and a white person, a Christian and an atheist, Jews and Muslims, if possible. We needed a businesswoman sitting next to a logger, a young person beside an old, and anything else that might keep the twelve jurors from coming together like the spokes of a wheel to form a unity against Dad. Mr. Aireys had said he would check their watches and note their baseball caps, their haircuts, their handbags. DUIs should be on the jury and people with perfect records. Some should be nervous, biting their fingernails all the way down and others should have meticulous manicures and clothes. As diverse a group as possible, he said. That's what we wanted. Mr. Aireys' job was to use all the information he'd gathered and also intuit their dispositions. Are they hard on themselves? Then they might be harder on the defendant, he reasoned.

"There isn't a single ideal juror for us," Mr. Aireys had explained. "But there is an ideal *jury*, as different an assortment as we can get. Motley, if it takes that. A rainbow of races and a quilt of everything else. No alliances when they go back to the juror room."

He said that Ms. Davies was going to try for people of like-types who would come together during deliberation. Her motto would be, "Unity means guilty. Diversity means acquittal." All white if she can get them, all from Albany or all from smaller towns, and so on. "She won't get that," Mr. Aireys had told us, "but if she gets enough with like-experiences and like-minds, it works against us."

That kind of talk scared me.

Mr. Aireys also had said that because this case was based on circumstantial evidence, not being able to form a "wheel" was *especially* important to us. There were going to be doubts about the evidence, and one or two persuasive spokes could turn the rest their way or brake them to a halt.

Could they rely on circumstantial evidence? I realized that was the key. We'd win or lose on that.

After a full week the jurors were finally seated. I thought they might run out of potential candidates, but they had the whole county to pull from, and everyone seemed eager to volunteer to do their civic duty. Too eager, I thought. Anyway, they now had their twelve and the alternates. Half men and half women. Some from small towns, some from Albany. An airline clerk and a hotel vice-president. A twenty-two-year-old and three jurors in their sixties. A trucker. A housewife. It was a pretty mixed bag, I thought. Mr. Aireys had done a good job. Now each of them will be asked to connect the dots. I hoped Mr. Aireys hadn't missed something important in anyone's past, something that could really hurt us.

All along I kept thinking there was no *real* evidence at all, nothing that could conclusively point to Dr. Simon Taylor as having killed my mom, Sunny. Everything was based on a "connect the dots" theory. That was good. But the handcuffs. Those might not be circumstantial evidence.

I was praying that they would be fair, even remembering Mom's favorite prayer: *Pritham Bhagautee simar kai Gur Nanak layee dhyaaye,* and saying — *ik ōaṅkār.*

I found myself praying hard.

21

Sometimes a cigar is only a cigar.
-Sigmund Freud

I Found This At The Library

"Let us say that a murder occurs. Miss X is found shot to death in her car. On the seat is a book with Mr. Y's fingerprints on them. His fingerprints are also on her cigarette pack and lighter. Cigarette butts of his brand are in the ashtray and his DNA is on them. These constitute circumstantial evidence of Mr. Y's presence in the car.

"But as with all circumstantial evidence, it is easy to make the wrong inference. It may well be that Miss X borrowed the book from Mr. Y. Perhaps they were close friends, colleagues, even lovers. They could have shared a cigarette upon meeting. Mr. Y, a gentleman, might have assisted Miss X in retrieving a cigarette from her pack, only to find it empty. He then gave her one of his own, lighting it for her while he held the cigarette with his lips before she went to her car.

"In that case the circumstantial evidence is insufficient to reach a conclusion.

"Most verdicts are based in whole or in part upon circumstantial evidence. The circumstances of a case will always influence the mind as

it forms a conclusion. In some instances the inference may be irresistible, but wrong. It requires an alert juror to see when an irresistible inference is too weak to be a deciding factor."
—James T. Weston, Esq.
Trying the Facts of the Case[23]

---

[23] Random House, 2009, Page 233

22

**I cannot think of any need in childhood as
strong as the need for a father's protection.
-Sigmund Freud**

"THANK YOU, YOUR HONOR. My opening remarks will be brief."

Ms. Davies turns to the jury.

"Thank you all for being here. You have made sacrifices to be here, and I thank you for that too, and for your participation as citizens."

She stands there a moment, as if enjoying the quiet in the courtroom and enjoying everyone's eyes upon her.

"I am honored to be here with you. You see, I am *your* lawyer. I am the lawyer for the people, all the people. My client is the state of New York, and you have given me a tremendous responsibility in trying this case. I am humbled, and I will do my utmost best."

She turns to my dad and points. "*That man committed a heinous crime.*"

She waits, still pointing. I know she is hoping my dad will look away. He just looks back at her calmly. No anger, no fear.

"Simon Taylor killed his wife. Her name was Sunny Taylor. How did he do it? Well, he handcuffed Sunny and he strangled her. And before or after he strangled her, he took Sunny to a wooded area to hide her body. It wasn't found for years. Nine years to be exact.

"Simon Taylor's wife, Sunny, was barely a skeleton when they found her. She still had the handcuffs on. Those handcuffs are a key point in this trial. They are unusual. They are unique. I will show you that no one else in the county, no one else in the whole state had the same unique handcuffs. Only one person did. Simon Taylor. Ladies and gentlemen of the jury, it's a simple matter of two plus two. Yes, two plus two. Please remember that.

"Simon Taylor had the unique handcuffs. Only him. He bought them, received them through the mail, and was seen with them. We have a witness to that. And Mrs. Taylor — Sunny — was found strangled and with the identical handcuffs on her.

"Now, no one saw Simon Taylor strangle Sunny. No one saw him take Sunny to the woods a mile away. So how do we know it was Simon Taylor, the same person sitting right over there? Two plus two. That's how we know. Two plus two.

"You may be thinking that that's only circumstantial evidence, and you are right. But that is what life is, a series of circumstances. Circumstantial evidence can be more powerful than even direct eyewitness evidence. *Often* it is more powerful, as in this case. Eye witnesses can be wrong, and very frequently are. But in this case the uniqueness of the handcuffs that only Simon Taylor owned sets them apart from any other handcuffs — only *he* had them. That's unmistakable.

"Let me give you an example of how circumstantial evidence works. Let's say you came out one morning and saw that your car was badly damaged from behind and there were skid marks leading right up to the damage. You'd conclude that the car with tires matching those skid marks is the same car that hit yours. You didn't see it, though. You didn't hear it, either. But it's still a fact. Two plus two. Then you find a neighbor's car with the same tire treads and a huge dent in the front of his car. There's still no smoking gun. No eye witness. Maybe it's all a coincidence. Maybe it was a different car that did it. Maybe a lot of other cars had the same tread and the same dent.

"But what if the tire treads are unique? Imported maybe, brought in especially from China. And the only person in the community, in the whole state, known to have those tires with those specific treads is your neighbor. And only your neighbor had the keys to his car that night, no one else. There was no evidence the car had been broken into, no evidence it had been stolen that night.

"Now what would you conclude? That's right. Two plus two.

"But the neighbor claims he knew nothing about it. Of course he does. Is that credible? He says that he's as concerned now about his car as you are about yours. Do you believe him? Do you trust him? Two plus two.

"Oh, and he had a nice family. A nice house. Was a nice person most of the time. Maybe even a doctor. With children. Does that matter, or does the evidence matter? The evidence always matters. Two plus two.

"Now a lot of you may have heard of Simon Taylor before. He's the famous psychiatrist who wrote a best-selling book. I've never read it, but I assume it is good. Maybe it is great. You may hear in this courtroom what a great father he is, what a terrific husband he was, and that he was a super shrink. But none of that matters. Two plus two matters, that's all.

"So let's imagine for a moment the best circumstances that we can. Let's imagine that Sunny's death was not intended. Simon Taylor and Sunny were making love as they liked it, with the handcuffs and whatever else, but something went wrong. One of them went too far. Certainly it wouldn't have been Sunny. It had to have been Simon Taylor who went too far. He was the one in control, wasn't he? Sunny was already subdued. In any event, afterward, Simon Taylor had to make her body disappear. It wasn't hard. There are back stairs and a back door, and the children are absorbed in their playing. So Simon Taylor somehow gets Sunny to the car, comes back and locks the door to make sure that the children are safe, and away he goes . . . to dispose of her body. To dispose of his wife, Sunny.

"If that were the case, it could be manslaughter, not murder. But that wasn't the case. This was intentional. This was murder. If Simon Taylor had loved his wife, he wouldn't have broken her neck, as the experts will testify happened. The good doctor wouldn't have hidden Sunny's body in the woods. Just left it out there, not even bothering to bury it or even cover it. If it had not been intentional, the good doctor would have reported it regardless of the publicity and the embarrassment. He would have seen to it that the wife he says he loved was given a proper burial and a proper period of mourning.

"But none of that happened. He didn't even take the handcuffs off her! That's what he really thought of her.

"Now what about motive? You will hear Mr. Aireys assert that there was no motive, and therefore Dr. Taylor could not have killed his wife. Two points: First, as a matter of law, we do not need to show a motive. Motive is not an element of the crime itself. What happened—the terrible, terrible murder of Sunny Taylor—is the only thing that is relevant here. You will see that clearly enough when we are done. Second, motives are often concealed. We all know that. That the motive is not apparent to us doesn't mean there wasn't one. Was Sunny having an affair? We don't know. Was Sunny leaving the defendant? Was she taking her children back home to India? We don't know. We don't know what else went on between them behind closed doors. But a motive was there. Clearly it was there or this tragedy, this terrible murder, never would have happened.

"This is an easy case. It's my easiest one in a long time. Of course Mr. Aireys over there will throw up smoke screens every other minute. You can expect that from him. He will try to hide the truth, throw reasonable doubt at you like a hundred marbles on the floor for you to slip on. But this is a simple case. The simplest of cases.

"In the end you will see that Dr. Simon Taylor — that man right over there — killed his wife, Sunny Taylor. I will show you that he handcuffed her and took her to that wooded area. I will show you that he strangled her. I will show you that it could *only* have been him and no one else. I will show you two and two. I will let you add them up. Two plus two is what matters. When you add them up, you'll find that you have four.

"Thank you."

23

**The suffering which comes from our relations to
other men is more painful than any other suffering.
-Sigmund Freud**

"THANK YOU MS. DAVIES. I certainly appreciate your example.
I think I'll even use it myself.

"Ladies and gentlemen of the jury, I too want to thank you for
being here today. I think you got an earful there. I hope it hasn't
unsettled you. Ms. Davies has tried to convince you that somehow the absence of evidence is itself evidence. That's right. There
is no evidence, nothing directly or even indirectly known about
who took the life of Sunny Taylor, Simon's wife. But to Ms.
Davies that's evidence. Of course that's nonsense.

"Ms. Davies even had to invent a little story. Okay, I'd like to
use the car example Ms. Davies gave us too; the skid marks and
the neighbor's car with the same unique tires.

"First, notice that Ms. Davies said that the neighbor was the
only person in the neighborhood with those tires that had a specific tread. Now, I try to imagine her going to every house in the
neighborhood and checking every car and every single tire. Of
course she didn't do that, assuming this was a real case, which it
wasn't of course. It was just a story.

"Nevertheless, Ms. Davies there would have deduced that the neighbor's car was the only car in the neighborhood with those specific tires. How would she get information like that? From some computers, I suppose. From tire dealers in the area. She would then be relying on those computer records to be proof, as if it were the only proof available to her.

"Did you also notice that she said those tires were the only *known* tires like that in the state? The only *known* ones? What about the *unknown* ones? Well, she obviously couldn't take those into account as even a possibility because it would destroy her handy theory. The unknowns. Already there is reasonable doubt and a lot of it.

"Specialty tires might be purchased out of state. Yes? We are near Massachusetts, Vermont, Pennsylvania, and the tires might have been bought at a specialty shop in one of those states and then driven or shipped here.

"Oh, but the accident to the front of the neighbor's car. Could it have happened a different way? Maybe. And that *maybe* is not two plus two. It is reasonable doubt. Reasonable doubt. It's zero plus zero. Ladies and gentlemen of the jury, there are people getting out of jail right now because it was later determined that the circumstantial evidence which convicted them was simply wrong. Flat wrong. Completely wrong. Please remember that.

"Now of course Ms. Davies' scenario was made up and ours here today is real. Dr. Simon Taylor is accused of doing something terrible, and yet he had no motive. Ms. Davies went on at length about some hidden motivation that we don't know of. Simon and Sunny were in love. There was no affair with anyone else. Ms. Davies can find none. But this *unknown* is supposed to be a factor in her favor. This *unknown* is her evidence. What Ms. Davies says she doesn't know is supposed to convict Dr. Taylor. But that's not what reasonable people think.

"Simon had no motive and he had no opportunity, and Ms. Davis will present none. Zero plus zero is . . . well, you know what it is. Dr. Taylor certainly had the means, as you'll see. But if he had no reason to do this to the woman he loved, and no opportunity at all, then how could he have done it? And why? It just doesn't make any sense. It doesn't make any sense because he didn't. He didn't do it.

"Here zero plus zero does not add up to four. Here it means Simon Taylor didn't do it at all, that he couldn't have done it, and that he had no reason to do it. Zero plus zero is the equation to keep in mind.

"One more thing. What Ms. Davies neglected to tell you is that when evidence is circumstantial, that means there is more than one explanation. That's what it *always* means. *Always.* Sunny, a terrific and beautiful person, was the love of Simon's life. She was the mother of his two children, one of whom is sitting right there behind him.

"Again, Simon had no motivation at all and no opportunity. There is zero. And zero means even more than reasonable doubt. It means he didn't do it. When we're done you'll see that there is so much reasonable doubt that it is so abundantly clear that Simon did not and could not have done this awful thing.

"The real tragedy is that whoever killed the woman Simon loved is still out there. Maybe it was a passerby at that time. Maybe it was someone from the neighborhood who took advantage of her. Maybe it was someone else. Who knows what else that person may have done in the years since then? We *don't* know.

"Ms. Davies was right about one thing. This *is* an easy case. Simon is as innocent as any of you are. You will see that in this courtroom.

"I want to thank you again, each of you individually. You and you, and you over there. Thank you for being here today."

"And thank you, Your Honor."

24

**First look into the depths of yourelf.
Then you will understand why this illness
was bound to come upon you.
-Sigmund Freud**

I WAS SUCH A MESS AS THE TRIAL BEGAN that my shoulders were shaking. I'd never felt such fear. Everything could be gone, not just my mom, but my dad too. I didn't trust Mr. Aireys and I didn't really understand everything that was going on. But at least Mr. Aireys had taken the prosecutor's own example and turned it around on her on the spot, broken it apart and made it seem doubtful. For the moment I loved him for it. But I didn't know how long that would last.

Ms. Davies' first witness was called. It was Trooper Reginald Wood. Mr. Aireys had told us that Trooper Wood would be there to set the scene for the jury, to let them know what had happened that day when Mom went missing.

Trooper Wood was retired and no longer in uniform, but he had on his black-rimmed glasses and he was still an imposing figure the way he moved to the stand. He remembered the incident about Mom quite clearly, and read extensively from the notes he made when he came to the house that day. What he didn't read he remembered quite vividly. He had the hour and minute that he arrived, the names of the neighbors, the time he came back with the scent dog, even the time that Grandpa Sam and Grandma Janet got there. Looking up from notes for a moment, he even remembered that they brought two bicycles for us. But there was nothing at all damaging for him to say.

I didn't realize that Ms. Davies was trying to make just one point. But she could make it only after Trooper Wood had answered all the questions she knew Mr. Aireys would ask later. It was her way of deflating them.

So she asked if Trooper Wood would confirm that my dad was upset, maybe confused and probably in shock. He replied *yes* to each of those. He admitted that Dad held nothing back, that he even offered his computer right away when they asked for it. Trooper Wood stated that Dad had searched with them to find Mom, and that for months after Mom was gone Trooper Wood still saw fresh posters with Mom's picture along his routes and on poles in different towns.

There was nothing against my dad, nothing at all. It was actually helping our case. Then Ms. Davies got to her point.

"Trooper Wood, do you recall searching the house when you first arrived."

"Yes, I do."

Trooper Wood looked directly at the jurors as he spoke. He hadn't forgotten the basics of being a good witness.

"And what did you find?"

"Nothing."

"No evidence of a break in?"

"Correct. None at all."

"No broken windows or doors forced?"

"Correct."

"No evidence that anyone had come in at all?"

"Correct."

"Based on your experience and what Simon Taylor said, and of course your common sense, would you conclude that nothing could have been stolen that day?"

"Well, at least nothing seemed to have been stolen through force that day. I can't say if anything was missing, as I had no access to the entire inventory of the house."

"Did Dr. Taylor say that anything was missing? A TV perhaps, or a stereo?"

"No."

"No money was gone?"

"Dr. Taylor did not report anything missing."

"If there had been anything else there, say handcuffs, might they have been stolen by someone?"

"I didn't know of the existence of any handcuffs, ma'am. There was simply no evidence of anything broken into. Dr. Taylor himself said that nothing was missing."

"So if handcuffs had been stolen that day and used by someone else on Sunny Taylor, you would have known about it?"

"Objection. Trooper Woods couldn't possibly have known what wasn't there."

"Sustained."

"Thank you, Trooper Wood. Your witness, Mr. Aireys."

It didn't get much better when Mr. Aireys got up there and had Trooper Wood simply restate most of what he had already said about Dad's concern and confusion, that Dad had been trying to understand what had happened and had actually become frantic.

"Would you say that Dr. Taylor displayed the demeanor and actions of a man who was in great distress?"

"Yes, I would."

"A man who is grieving and not hiding anything, Trooper Wood?"

"The actions, yes, but a person can be a good actor."

"In your opinion based on more than twenty-five years on the force, was Simon Taylor acting?"

"No sir. I don't think he was."

"Thank you."

"Redirect, Your Honor."

"Yes, go ahead Ms. Davies."

"Trooper Wood, have you ever been fooled by someone who said they didn't do something?"

"Yes, ma'am, I suppose I have."

"Just once?"

"That would be fortunate, ma'am, if it was just once."

"Thank you."

Trooper Wood stepped down and went to the back of the courtroom where he somehow found a seat. He was going to stay.

The next witness was a Dr. Hodges, the medical examiner who had gone to the woods where Mom was found and where he had examined her and took pictures even before she was brought back to his morgue. The pictures would be of a skeleton with long hair, a silver barrette containing the inscription *Ik ōaṅkār*, and the hinged handcuffs around the skeleton's wrists.

He was going to testify about the cervical fracture of Mom's neck, the larvae feces found in the remains of the abandoned wasp nest on my mom, which was how Dr. Hodges identified the approximate year Mom was put there, along with other things.

I didn't stay for it. I went outside and sat on a bench.

The testimony of Dr. Hodges went on until the lunch break and it still wasn't done even then. At noon, the morning session was finished. The judge instructed everyone to be back after lunch at one thirty. One of Mr. Aireys' assistants, Elena, pushed through the crowd ahead of my dad, smiling and smiling to everyone. Dad saw me out front waiting for him and managed a smile and a small wave. Reporters were trying to ask him questions. There was a microphone set up in case he wanted to speak. He didn't. He pushed his way over to me and said we'd go somewhere for lunch.

Somehow Christy Jones' family got out ahead of Dad. They were holding up the sign and glaring at us. Grandpa Sam quickly caught up with us and tried to stay between us and them. They looked grim and desolate, just standing there waving the sign, until I ran over to them and shouted, "Get out of here you freaks! My dad didn't do *anything!*" They backed up but I kept coming. Grandpa Sam tried to pull me away but another burst came from inside me — "*You're fucking wrong!* "

Grandpa Sam grabbed me hard and spun me around and tried to hold me against him but I kept screaming.

"Don't!" he shouted sharply after wrestling me away. Then I started to cry. Grandpa shoved me over to Dad who held me in his arms. "You're okay, baby," he said. "You're okay."

I was so glad Grandma Janet was back at the house with Veronica and Rainbow that day because then she couldn't tell us about how God was going to intervene. I didn't need another recommendation to go to the nearest Catholic Church and ask the statues to watch over us right then. As it turned out, Grandma Janet the Saint-in-Waiting had dragged Veronica out with her that morning to go to Hudson, which had become her favorite town to ring doorbells and make her announcements about where the nearest church is and how crossing yourself with holy water reduced your sentence in purgatory.

I didn't want to be in any church. I didn't expect any imaginary help from an imaginary god. Yet I thought about *Wahaguru* and Guru Nanak, and hoped that Mom's faith would somehow help. But I knew that wasn't going to happen either. From somewhere deep inside me I knew that we were on our own.

I was still shaking as we took our afternoon lunch together at Peaches Café. I ordered a salad and the Mediterranean grilled something-or-other. Grandpa Sam the Bicycle Man had coffee and a salad. So did Dad. Mr. Aireys ordered a huge hamburger. Rachel and Elena were both apparently dieting for some reason and had small salads. We sat in a corner.

I looked from Dad to Mr. Aireys. Neither looked especially happy. I didn't ask, but Dad did say that the medical examiner's testimony would continue through the afternoon. I wanted him to tell me that he was pleased with Mr. Aireys work that morning after I went outside, at least to calm me down, but he didn't. I imagined it was more of Mr. Aireys' staging of objections and sidebars so that the jurors might think something important was being kept back from them, something that might point directly to Dad's innocence. Every little bit counted.

After the food arrived everyone but me and Dad started in on the meal. Nobody spoke. Then Dad put both hands on the table and made an announcement.

"I'm going to testify."

Mr. Aireys went right on eating as if nothing had been said.

"I mean it. I'm going to testify."

"Good, Dad. I think you should."

Mr. Aireys glanced sideways at me, then went back to his meal.

Grandpa Sam spoke up. "Son, you better listen to Mr. Aireys. You listen to him."

"Good, Dad," I said again. "Don't listen to him."

Another glance from Mr. Aireys, but he said nothing, though I noticed his assistants stiffen and glance sideways at him several times. Mr. Aireys just went on eating. His assistants then continued eating too, but Dad and I just waited. Finally Mr. Aireys was done. He wiped his mouth and folded his napkin.

"We'll talk," he said, as if to nobody in particular.

"No," I insisted. "Dad's going to take the stand."

Mr. Aireys asked for the check.

There was no more talk that day about Dad taking the stand. I waited outside through the afternoon, taking a couple of walks around the block and doing some window-shopping. My mind was everywhere else; on Mom, the handcuffs, my dad, Veronica, Ms. Davies, Mr. Aireys' little tactics. Was I not seeing something? Was I not admitting something to myself? Maybe I should have been inside the courtroom all along. I might have seen something in the pictures that could have helped.

At the end of the day Dad came out a side door with Grandpa Sam, saying nothing to the reporters. He gave me his little wave and Grandpa Sam made sure to run over before I could cause more trouble. But we had avoided the Jones' and their sign. We walked to the courthouse parking lot.

I drove us home that night. Dad seemed especially preoccupied so I had offered to drive. Dad knew how good a driver I was for a young person, and besides, Grandpa Sam couldn't drive because of some eye problems at dusk.

As I stopped at the toll booth on I-90 Dad looked over at me. Grandpa Sam was in back. Dad waited a moment until I took the ticket. He turned toward me.

"I'm going to fire him," Dad said.

"Good," I said.

"Damn it, son. Don't you dare."

"I have to."

"Do it, Dad."

"No you don't, son. You listen to him. You listen to me."

"Then who will we get?" I asked.

"I don't know. Maybe I'll just get up there and testify, and that will be all we need to do. There isn't much of a defense for me, except who I am. That's all we have because everything else points to me. I just don't understand it. I don't understand how all of this could happen."

I nodded my agreement.

"I'm going to get up there and let them see who I am. I don't need Aireys."

Grandpa Sam leaned forward and started up about how Dad was a damn fool if he didn't listen to Mr. Aireys. Dad turned around to answer him, but then the car behind us honked loudly. In the mirror I saw Grandpa Sam turn and growl something at the driver.

I quickly drove forward, and we went the rest of the way home in silence.

25

**A certain degree of neurosis is of inestimable value as a drive, especially to a psychologist.
-Sigmund Freud**

"**Ms. ANITA ROGERS,** please come forward."

Dad's former secretary is an attractive brunette who is now in her mid-forties. She's dressed modestly for court, in a simple white blouse and dark slacks. No jewelry, no lipstick, wearing only a little make-up. As she passes Dad on her way to the stand, she turns toward him with compressed lips. She doesn't want to testify, but she has to. Anita is sworn in.

She says what Mr. Aireys told us she'd say: that around the time Dad had quit his practice she had gone into his office to help him organize his files, knowing that no patients were there, and had noticed the handcuffs on his desk.

Ms. Rogers' demeanor is stiff as she testifies, and her mouth quivers more than once. She says the handcuffs were beside a blue box. She describes the handcuffs in a way that makes it clear they were identical to the ones found on Mom.

"And what did you say to Dr. Taylor about them?"

"I made a little joke, was all. I said, 'Did a patient leave those behind?' or something like that."

"And did Dr. Taylor answer you?"

"Yes. He said, 'Everybody needs something, Anita.'"

"What did you take that to mean?"

"Objection, Anita Rogers is not a mind reader."

"I didn't ask her to read Mr. Taylor's mind, just to tell us what his statement meant to her."

"Sustained. Move on, Ms. Davies."

"Did you ever see those handcuffs again?"

"No, I didn't."

"So, Simon Taylor could have taken the handcuffs home that night. Is that correct?"

"Objection. The handcuffs could have flown to the moon too, but they didn't. Ms. Rogers wouldn't know it if they had. Calls for a conclusion beyond the scope of her personal knowledge."

"Sustained."

"If the handcuffs had remained in the office, might you have seen them?"

"Yes, I might have, but I didn't go looking through Dr. Taylor's file cabinets. He was strict about patient confidentiality."

"No more questions, Your Honor."

"Mr. Aireys? You may proceed."

"Ms. Rogers, hello. How long were you Dr. Taylor's secretary?"

"About five years. I was the only secretary he ever had."

"Did you like Dr. Taylor?"

"Of course. Everyone did."

"Did he seem unstable to you?"

"Objection. Dr. Taylor's the psychiatrist, Your Honor. Not the witness."

"Sustained."

"Given what you know from your experiences in life, did Dr. Taylor seem any different from any other normal person you know?"

"He was nicer, and sometimes funnier. He was very generous too."

"Did you ever see him do anything strange?"

"Oh, no sir."

"Maybe get angry at a patient or very frustrated?"

"I never saw Dr. Taylor angry at anyone. But I'm sure he got frustrated sometimes with patients. They could be quite a lot to deal with. At least it seemed so to me."

"No other questions, Your Honor. I want to thank the witness for coming."

"Redirect, Your Honor?"

"Go ahead, Ms. Davies."

"Ms. Rogers, did Dr. Taylor ever tell you why he was interested in psychiatry?"

"No, he never said."

"He was mostly interested in phobias when he started, isn't that right?"

"And obsessions. That's what part of his practice was about, phobias and obsessions, trying to help people. His book too, at least some of it."

"You've read his book?"

"Yes, of course."

"Were there any mirrors in his office?"

"Objection. No relevance whatsoever."

"Let's see where this goes, Mr. Aireys. Overruled."

"Go on, Ms. Rogers. Were there any mirrors in the office?"

"I don't think so. Come to think of it, there weren't any."

"Was there a bathroom?"

"Yes, down the hall."

"Was there a mirror in there?"

"Yes, of course."

"And Dr. Taylor used that bathroom?"

"No, he had one in his office."

"Was there a mirror in there?"

"I don't know. A cleaning lady would come in during the night. I never went into his personal bathroom."

"Are you aware of any phobias Dr. Taylor had?"

"Objection! Relevance."

"Thank you, Ms. Rogers."

"The Court thanks the witness. You may step down."

I had no idea why Ms. Davies asked the last questions. Dad's mirror problem had never been mentioned outside our home. How did the prosecution know? Mr. Aireys had no idea about the mirror phobia and was giving Dad a strange look. He started to lean over to ask Dad what was going on and then abruptly stopped. He would ask about it later.

Then I remembered the mirrors in the courthouse lobby, two tall ones opposite the inside pillars when you come in. I'd see Dad always make a quick left through the door to avoid them, taking the stairs instead of the elevator. I always went with him up the stairs, though everyone else, even Mr. Aireys and his assistants, took the elevator. It's normal for someone to glance at himself briefly when passing the mirrors, adjusting a tie or brushing off shoulders, smiling for a moment to check how he looks.

I figured Ms. Davies and her team had watched Dad come into the courthouse. They'd seen him avoid the mirrors. Even the people who took the stairs would sometimes stop at one of the mirrors first. Not Dad.

Okay, so Ms. Davies had guessed about Dad's mirror phobia. It meant nothing and had nothing to do with what happened to Mom.

But about the mirrors, it wasn't over.

After lunch the judge recessed the court for the rest of the day because one of the jurors had gotten sick, probably in the court cafeteria. I'm sure the personal injury lawyers were hovering over her when they heard she passed out or was flailing on the floor. If that's what happened.

I drove Dad home after the mirror phobia was brought up. We were alone; Grandpa Sam the Bicycle Man had stayed with Veronica so Grandma Janet and two friends from Church could do their Hudson evangelizing. After reading Freud, I understand now that Grandma suffers from hagiomania. It's a mania that drives one to want to become a saint. As the trial was progressing, she was going door to door more often. Maybe she thought her work could save Dad too.

On the way home I told Dad how I thought they figured out the mirror thing.

"It doesn't matter, baby," he said. "It's nothing."

"It'll be reported in the papers."

Dad shrugged. "What matters is what happened to your Mom. What matters is the truth, that's all."

Each day, on the drive home, we'd pass blueberry and raspberry farms. That afternoon I pulled into a farm that sells little baskets of berries for three dollars, or you can pick your own for two dollars a basket. Dad didn't say anything when I stopped. He just got out of the car and handed the woman a twenty-dollar bill and said we were going to pick our own and eat them in the field. That's what we did. Dad took off his suit jacket and rolled up his sleeves. I was wearing a dark skirt and cream blouse. We bent over a row, side by side, and picked and ate, stuffing ourselves. We didn't talk, but we couldn't help smiling all the while. In no time we had red fingers and lips and smears all over us. Still we didn't talk, just a lot of *ooohs*, and *oh my's*.

For a time the world was back on track. I imagined Mom at home, waiting for us.

26

**Sadism is all right in its place,
but it should be directed to proper ends.
-Sigmund Freud**

THAT NIGHT I MADE DINNER. Not the usual frozen turkey plate, but something much better. I had gone to the store and bought some pasta, fresh tomatoes, and garlic. Dad and I would have a feast. We'd have the place to ourselves because Grandpa Sam and Grandma Janet had taken Veronica into Cobleskill for a movie she wanted to see. I poured Dad two fingers of Scotch adding two cubes, the way he liked it, and set everything on the table. I was the woman of the house. The one who really cares.

Later, the phone rang. It was Mr. Aireys. He wanted Dad to explain about the mirrors. I listened as Dad said it was an insignificant phobia he'd developed a long time ago, something he had dealt with as an adult, and that it wasn't an issue.

"No," Dad said, anger rising in his voice. "It won't make me look unstable. Especially when I take the stand."

I could hear Mr. Aireys's voice through the phone. Dad held the phone at a distance from his ear and winked at me. When Mr.

Aireys was done screaming, Dad said, "Withdraw if you want. I don't care. I want the jury to see who I am. I want my chances with them."

There was more shouting then, but after a while Mr. Aireys seemed to calm down. He didn't want to give up the case. It would look bad for him, and besides, a win or mistrial would be one more notch in his belt.

The next day the sick juror was back, and the trial proceeded. The vice president of Chinese Bazaar took the stand, a woman named Elva Lewis. She was an accountant-type, late thirties, tight-faced with half-rim glasses and her hair in a bun, someone who might literally let her hair down at night and look totally different. I wanted to lean over and tell Dad that I thought she needed his twice-a-day remedy, anything to get a smile out of him, but I was afraid that if anyone overheard me, somehow it would hurt Dad. He didn't look good.

Elva Lewis testified that she was the company's sales manager, treasurer, secretary, and agent for process. She spoke about the structure of the company and provided the name of the president who was a Chinese entrepreneur living in Taiwan. She said Chinese Bazaar imported items from manufacturers in China and the Philippines, and sold them on the Internet and through mail order catalogues in different countries. She explained the focus of their products — mostly hand weapons, such as swords, batons, nun chucks, and blackjacks. She said that they also sold items that are usually used for defense and restraint, such as body armor and handcuffs.

Ms. Davis handed Elva Lewis the handcuffs that were found on Mom so Miss Lewis could inspect them.

"Miss Lewis, does your company sell these handcuffs?"

"Yes, we do."

"And what is their model number?

"H4509-L."

"Are you the exclusive supplier?"

"That's our agreement with the manufacturer."

"Objection. The witness didn't answer the question."

"Are you the exclusive supplier?"

"As far as we know, yes."

"And what are these made out of?"

"Mostly steel. They're not nickel, though they look like they are."

"Do you sell other handcuffs like these?"

"You mean with hinges?"

"Yes, with hinges."

"I think we have three or four different models with hinges, but these are the only ones with three hinges and a dragon-etching on them. The dragons are etched by hand, so each pair is a little different from the others."

"Thank you. Does the dragon have any significance here? Any purpose?"

"No functional purpose of course, just decoration. It makes the handcuffs look different from the plain ones, that's all. Because the etchings are done by hand, each pair is unique. Collectors usually want things that are different and rare. The three hinges are different, and the dragon is quite different."

"When did Chinese Bazaar start selling these, Model H4509-L?"

"Back in 2000."

"Can you tell us how they were packaged?"

"They would have been sent in a cobalt-blue box wrapped in a plain paper."

"Can you tell us how many you've sold?"

"Not many. Maybe two hundred pairs."

"Why so few?"

"The manufacturer packages them three to a box. Collectors, as well as those who buy them for restraint, usually want just one pair. Buying the box set costs two hundred and fifty dollars, and that's a lot of money."

"Of the two hundred you've sold so far, how many were sold prior to August, 2005?"

"Just eight. Our company was still pretty new then and not doing much business yet."

"Have you checked your records to see where these eight were shipped?"

"Yes I have. Five boxes were purchased by a gentleman in Thailand, two boxes went to Mexico, and one to the United States?"

"Just one box to the United States, are you sure?"

"Yes."

"What state were they shipped to?"

"New York."

"To what city were they shipped?"

"New York City."

"What address?"

"I have it here. Let me see, 181 West Seventy-Ninth Street."

"Is there an office number?"

"Number 1C."

"The name of the person you shipped the box of handcuffs to?"

"Dr. Simon Taylor. At that address."

"Thank you Miss Lewis. Counselor?"

Mr. Aireys rose and approached her. "Miss Lewis, were you with the company back in 2000 when the company started selling the handcuffs?"

"No, I was hired in 2009."

"Who had your job back then?"

"I don't know her name."

"You've never met her?"

"No, the company has changed a lot since I came on board."

"But you still have the records from before you were hired?"

"Yes, they're still available."

"Though you can't personally verify their accuracy."

"Personally, no."

"And you can't verify that there are no other suppliers that you don't know about before you were hired, can you?"

"No, I can't."

"So the company from which you purchased the handcuffs could be selling to other companies as well as to yours."

Ms. Davies rose to her feet. "Objection, Your Honor. Is there a question?"

"I'm sorry. Miss Lewis, is it possible that the company which you purchase the handcuffs from could be selling to other companies and not just yours?"

"That's not our arrangement with them."

"That's not what I asked."

"Yes, I guess it's possible."

"In fact, are you aware of other companies that have sold around you, to other buyers and distributors?"

"I guess I am."

"I'll take that as a 'yes.' Now, you said that only eight of this type of handcuff were sold prior to 2005, isn't that correct?"

"That's correct."

"But you really meant to say eight boxes of three pair in each."

"Yes, I'm sorry."

"Did you say that five boxes were shipped to Thailand and two to Mexico?"

"Yes."

"Did you say that collectors usually want just one pair?"

"Yes, that's correct."

"And that they usually want only one pair, those who want them for restraints?"

"Yes."

"Can you tell us how many of those boxes that went to Thailand and Mexico were split up and then resold after arriving?"

"You mean, that the purchaser resold some and kept one pair for himself?"

"Yes, that's what I mean. How many were split up?"

"I can't possibly know that, sir."

"So your records do not account for what happened after the boxes arrived at each destination."

"Your Honor, what's the question?" It was Ms. Davies.

"Sustained. Ask the question Mr. Aireys.

"Ms. Lewis, can you account for what happened to each of the three pairs in each of the eight boxes — twenty four pairs of handcuffs in all — after they arrived at the purchasers' addresses?"

"No, I cannot."

"Don't customers sometimes resell things they've purchased from you?"

"I'm sure some do."

"So back then, there were as many as twenty-four separate pairs out there, not including the ones you claim that your company sent to Simon Taylor."

"Yes, I suppose so."

"They could be anywhere, isn't that so?"

"I suppose."

"Thank you, Miss Lewis. No more questions for this witness, Your Honor. None at all."

The holes Mr. Aireys' punched in Miss Lewis's testimony weren't very large, and everyone knew that, but he did the best he could to raise some doubt about the accuracy of the records and to suggest that individual pairs may have been resold.

"What do you think, sweetie?" my dad asked me later when we were sitting at a restaurant eating lunch, just me and Dad this time. I was eating a grilled cheese as Dad had coffee. He sipped it and asked me again. "What do you think?"

"I think we'll win, Dad."

"Do you really?"

"I can't imagine anything else."

"I can't either. But sometimes our imaginations are too limited. I think anything can happen, Annie. I've already put the house up for sale, just in case."

"I don't care about the house. Are you going to take the stand?"

"I am. Mr. Aireys is going to start prepping me tonight."

"When are you going to do it?" I asked. "Take the stand."

"I'm not sure. Trooper Wood and Dr. Hodges and Anita have finished testifying, unless Mr. Aireys wants to bring them back. I don't think we'll hear more from the Chinese Bazaar woman. The Visa guy is next. Ms. Davies will bring in my credit card statement for the jury to see. It's a bit of overkill because they've already established that I'm pretty much the only person who had a pair of . . . them. Two plus two, like Davies said. I'm afraid it looks like two plus two to me too."

"What happened to zero plus zero?"

"The jury could easily believe that any motive had to do with something between your mom and me that isn't known, and that there was an opportunity."

Dad looked worse than I had seen him since Mom died.

"I think we're sunk," he said quietly. "Who do you think did it, Annie?"

"I don't know. I wish Mom were here. I wish she could tell everyone what happened. Then the jury would see the truth. Mom could save us."

In the final week of the trial, just days before the jury was sent out to deliberate, Dad found me crying in my room. He sat down next to me and somehow pulled my teenage body onto his lap. Then he started crying too. We both shook and shook and when we stopped crying and the storm had passed, Dad smiled and asked me to help him make dinner. He told me that we will struggle on. We had been eating a lot of frozen turkey during the trial. Now Dad and I microwaved it together, laughing as we called the other Chef Daddy and Chef Annie. Then Dad went into his awful French accent and used expressions like *chef-d'œu-vre* and *cuisinier*, and then tried to say a whole sentence in French. It came out garbled; something about the carrots being on a train.

I laughed so hard I fell down on the floor.

27

**What we call happiness comes from the sudden satisfaction of needs which have been dammed up to a high degree.
-Sigmund Freud**

RIGHT AFTER WE MOVED INTO OUR HOUSE IN WINDHAM, my mom got a little wooden birdhouse and hung it on the back porch. It's still there. I remember it was spring, and the birdhouse was quickly occupied by a small grayish-brown avian family. We had to be careful when we went out the back door so as not to upset the mother bird who would make harsh chirping calls to protect her eggs. Or maybe it was her nestlings she was protecting. It was hard to tell because the hole of the birdhouse was so small. The little bird would swoop out of the teeny hole, cackling at us as she flew by and land on the porch railing with her beak open wide, screaming.

That's the way I felt about what was happening. I was going to do everything a nineteen-year-old could do to protect my dad.

Mom's photographs are still all over the house. My favorite is the one where she's at the beach, her thick hair was loose and whirling behind her, her great eyes are alight, like two sparks. I loved it when her hair was loose, falling over her back like a dark curtain. There's also a picture that Dad took of her in bed on a Sunday morning. I had just brought in some eggs and toast and orange juice on a tray. Veronica was on the bed bouncing beside her. Mom's laughing hard. Dad's bedroom has pictures of their wedding and honeymoon, and pictures of when Mom was pregnant with Veronica and me. The pictures in the living room are of all of us together; they were snapshots that Mom had enlarged. But no studio pictures. Mom didn't like anything staged.

During the trial Dad and I talked about Mom and about how *determined* she was. Dad likes telling the story of the first time he had to bail her out of jail. We always laugh as hard as we can. Not only was Mom leading a march on an abortion clinic in the City, she was the *only* one in the march. An army of one. Mom was very Green—anti-nuke and anti-war, but abortions made her nuts; she believed they were a crime and should be illegal.

Like I said, Mom led a march-of-one outside the clinic, carrying a rolled up cardboard megaphone. Borrowing the line from the famous John Lennon song, she sang: *All we are saying, is give them a chance.* On her third day of peacefully protesting on the Second Avenue sidewalk, singing beautifully, someone called in a complaint that she was being a nuisance and obstructing the sidewalk. Officers were called in. Of course, Mom wasn't obstructing anyone, though I'll bet she was singing loudly. Mom used to sing at home, hymns or soft chants; we loved hearing her. It was *Mom*. But the folks in the clinic weren't enjoying listening to her.

Dad told me that the police weren't able to stop Mom's protest because of her First Amendment rights and because she wasn't a danger to anyone. She ignored the officers and kept right on singing—*All we are saying, is give them a chance.* People stopped to watch her; some were sympathetic or charmed, and began singing with her. That's when one of the officers tried to take the cardboard megaphone from Mom so she would acknowledge him. She accidentally stepped on his toe. Okay, probably not accidentally. She probably stomped on it. Like I said, *determined*.

I'm sure Dad wasn't smiling when he had to go to the police station, but he was smiling as he recounted the story again, and laughing at having to go to the women's holding center to post a small bond. He said that some of the police officers there were laughing about it. They had come to like Mom in the short time they knew her. But she had injured one of their own, and they had to do something. I imagine the officer whose toe she stomped as a burly guy with an Irish accent, though it could have been a small officer. I don't really know, but I prefer to think he was burly and Irish and regularly took down pimps and punks and dealers.

Dad said there was a hearing the next day and Mom had to promise the judge she wouldn't go back to the abortion clinic for ninety days, and that she would restrain herself from "perpetrating any further violence in the City." Then she was released to go home. What the judges didn't know was that she was already planning to protest at the Indian Point nuclear site on those next weekends. She got arrested there too. This time she carried a sign along with her megaphone, and the sign read, "Intercourse Nukes." Mom didn't like vulgarity. There was security at the site. They made her move down the road, so she took her protest there, a battalion of one.

But then some workers from the site approached her and said some things that weren't so nice. According to my smiling Dad, after the sign *fell* on one of them, they called the police. Another visit to a detention center and Dad had to get her out again. Dad said he was taking care of me that day, so I went with him, though I was too young to remember. Getting pregnant with Veronica put an end to Mom's demonstrations and arrests, but not to her grievances, of course.

I never saw my mom furious. Only once did I see her even half angry, and that was the time I had been going through her things.

The expert witness testimonies were next, and then the prosecution would rest. Mr. Aireys had told us that when the prosecution finished presenting its case, he would ask for a "directed verdict," which he explained is a request that the judge dismiss everything because Ms. Davies hadn't proven the charges. Even if the directed verdict isn't granted, it could be considered on appeal.

Christy's parents were still at the courthouse each day. I grew angrier every time I saw them. I hoped for an opportunity when I could tear up their stupid sign. I also heard they were speaking on the news a lot—though the TV wasn't on in our home at all now. In the courtroom Mrs. and Mr. Jones still looked old and angry.

Each expert had his time on the stand, though there wasn't all that much to say about the handcuffs or the Visa statement. There wasn't much for Mr. Aireys to oppose.

"Have your reviewed the credit card statement of Dr. Simon Taylor for February of 2004?"

"Yes I have."

"Can you tell us if the defendant made a purchase during that month that could be related to this case?"

They testified that the handcuffs had been purchased online, were then mailed on a certain date, and would have arrived in March of 2004, a year and seven months before Mom was missing.

Much of the court time was spent on Mr. Aireys finagling sidebars. He demanded a mistrial, which he was famous for. The judge was growing irritated.

After lunch the handcuff expert's testimony took up the whole afternoon. It was tedious but I wasn't going to miss any of it, not even for bathroom breaks, which I really needed.

Mr. Aaron Timmons had been an ex-narcotics investigator for NYPD and a lecturer at a number of police academies. The prosecutor had brought him all the way from Indianapolis where he had moved after he retired. He now specializes in commercial security and also owns a gun and ammo store. Ms. Davies established him as an expert who is familiar with all types of weapons and handcuffs, as well as how each is used. He even knows how to handcuff a one-armed man.

"Mr. Timmons, had you seen handcuffs like these before this case?"

"Only in pictures. They aren't typical."

"In what way aren't they typical?"

"The main thing is that the cuffs are a bit oval, and there are hinges rather than chain links between them."

"Anything else?"

"They have an etching on them. A dragon, it looks like."

"How are these different from typical handcuffs?"

"They're very different from the police type."

"In what ways?"

"Police handcuffs have swinging arms that go in two directions. They can be slapped on someone from either side quite easily. You can't do that with these."

"You mean, you can put these handcuffs on from only one direction?"

"Correct."

"What could handcuffs with these types of hinges be used for?"

"Objection."

"Overruled."

"Personal use, I guess. Some people buy them for looks. Collectors."

"What other types of personal use?"

"Objection, Your Honor. Mr. Timmons could go on all day with his speculations about other uses. We submit that handcuffs like these are used all the time in role-playing scenarios. Mr. Timmons can't possibly know all the ways they might be used."

"Sustained, this time."

"No other questions, Mr. Timmons. Thank you."

Mr. Aireys began his cross-examination.

"Mr. Timmons, thank you for coming all the way from Indianapolis."

"Sure."

"Is it illegal to own these handcuffs?"

"No, not at all."

"You said that these are an unusual pair, and not practical for law enforcement work, isn't that correct?"

"Yes, in my view."

"And that's because it's hard to put them on someone who's struggling, is that right?"

"Yes, and also because of the weight."

"Have you ever seen handcuffs like these that were used by a kidnapper?"

"No. Never until this case."

"Have you ever seen them on a dead body?"

"Never, until this case."

"But you have seen other kinds of handcuffs on a dead body?"

"Yes, a number of times."

"In your opinion, might you never have seen this type of handcuffs in a kidnapping or on a dead body because the two people using this model might each do so willingly?"

"That could be."

"So one person would have to put the handcuffs on the other person, and the other person would have to accept them willingly?"

"Probably, yes."

"And maybe the object of the game the two are playing is to control the other person's hands."

"It could be."

"Thank you, Mr. Timmons. Your Honor, we have no further questions."

The prosecution rested.

Mr. Aireys made his request for a directed verdict.

The judge quickly denied it, and the defense was directed to begin arguing its side at 8:00 Monday morning.

Dad had persuaded Mr. Aireys to let him take the stand, but that night at our home Mr. Aireys was having second thoughts. The circumstantial evidence against Dad was so shaky, he told us as we were seated around the kitchen table again, and parts of the testimony were so inconclusive, that some of the jury members might well be going Dad's way already; and, we needed only one juror to see reasonable doubt. Dad stroked Rainbow's ear and reminded Mr. Aireys of what everyone knows: "If the accused doesn't step up and speak, he looks guilty, isn't that right? Silence works against him, even if he has the right not to speak."

"You don't understand, Simon," Mr. Aireys said.

"I *do* understand," Dad countered.

"Good, Dad," I said sternly. Mr. Aireys stiffened and glared at me.

"That prosecutor is really good, Simon. I won't be responsible for the outcome."

Dad was adamant. He was going to speak. If Mr. Aireys objected he'd fire him. That was that.

Now it's Sunday, and Dad's sitting at the table with legal books and papers around him. "Where did you get all those?" I ask him.

Dad tells me he went to the law library over in Schoharie and is studying some relevant cases from the last two decades. I glance down at the tiny print. "About handcuffs, Dad?"

"About a lot of things, baby. I want to understand as much as I can."

Dad hasn't spoken to me about the handcuffs, but now says, "Sit down, sweetheart." Maybe this time he will tell me.

I sit opposite him at the table. "Can you tell me?" I ask.

Dad looks blankly at the pages, not reading them.

"Tell me," I say again and wait. "I know that people do things, Dad. I'm not so young."

"Don't doubt us, Annie. Your mom and me."

"I won't, Dad. I mean I *don't*."

He continues to stare down at the papers.

"You're reading about handcuffs?" I ask again. I take a breath and ask, "Are you going to tell me about Mom? Are you going to tell me what really happened?"

Dad folds his hands and sits back. He looks at me.

"I don't know what happened," he says softly. "Baby, if I did, I would tell you."

The next day it was Mr. Aireys' turn, and he put a number of forensic pathologists on the stand who said they couldn't be sure when Mom had died. I hated thinking about the abandoned wasp nest that had been built on her. The forensic pathologists had analyzed it and said the nest might be from the year after Dad reported Mom missing, maybe even later. Because of extreme climate swings, the experts could only approximate. Mr. Aireys informed the jury that an approximate date just wasn't good enough. Mom could have been taken to the woods at any time by practically anyone. He asked why the police hadn't found her years before when they had searched the area. It was a good question, with no good answer. But it wasn't very convincing.

Dad was to take the stand the next day. That morning as he came down the stairs, he seemed happier than I'd seen him in some time. Even Rainbow seemed happier for some reason, not asking to go out to the creek, but bouncing around in front of Dad as he went over his notes again while I cooked some ham and eggs. Later Dad shaved with his electric razor, and I checked his face to make sure he hadn't missed any spots. I chose his tie too, and after eliminating the yellow one and the red one, I picked one that's dark blue with little red stars on it. Blue seemed lucky to me. Stars are really positive. No other reasons than that. Well, that and I knew the tie would look really nice on him when he got up to testify.

Dad said I could drive the Saab. Once in the car he pointed to the top. "Up or down?" he asked, then without waiting for an answer said to himself, "Why not?"

He pressed the button and the top lifted quietly and packed itself under the rear deck. Dad smiled and leaned back in the passenger seat. It was still early morning and the air was brisk, but I didn't care. I didn't even put the heater on. I was with Dad, and everything was going to be okay.

Even before we were out of the driveway Dad turned on the radio. We'd never agreed much on music. He doesn't like Adele or Katy Perry or the Beastie Boys, and I don't like just about anything he likes. But over time we've agreed on the Beatles and some Pink Floyd, so when we're together we usually turn on the sixties station. But today he could listen to whatever he liked. Dad immediately punched the button for "True Oldies" on WVKZ, and amazingly, the song playing was, "It's a Beautiful Morning" by The Rascals. Dad actually sang along:

> . . . I think I'll go outside for a while, and just SMILE.

He didn't usually sing in the car. It was a really positive sign. He looked wonderfully handsome to me, but not as finely tailored as Mr. Aireys would be. Dad had circles under his eyes, but he still looked terrific.

Then we are in the courtroom and I'm sitting with Grandpa Sam behind Dad and Mr. Aireys. Dad is called to the witness stand. He rises and faces the clerk. She swears him in. Dad turns and winks at me. His Santa Claus eyes are shiny and bright.

Mr. Aireys smiles at Dad as if testifying has been part of the plan all along. The jury members are as awake as I've seen them. The room is really quiet.

Mr. Aireys' first job is to make Dad look as good as possible — open, honest, and straightforward. Mr. Aireys will have to ask some tough questions because the prosecution is sure going to. If Mr. Aireys asks them first, and in the right way, it will help defuse any problems.

Now Dad is on the stand. Mr. Aireys approaches him. The courtroom is still. Dad's testimony is rehearsed to a T. Mr. Aireys and I know exactly what to expect, exactly what Dad is going to say.

We are wrong.

PART III

28

Love and work. Work and love.
That's all there is.
-Sigmund Freud

THE NIGHT BEFORE DAD TOOK THE STAND I went to his room and got into bed beside him. The reading lamp was on and he was sitting up looking through more legal things. I pulled his blanket over me too and lay on my side facing him. Dad already knew what he was going to do the next day, but I didn't.

I told him that when this was all over I was going to start up Mom's garden again. When we moved in she had begun a garden on the south side of the house. She got some gloves and digging tools and she planted seeds that were going to be bouquets of spinach and red-leaf lettuce. She planted asparagus too, and some carrots and beets, though no one in our house ever ate beets. I remember trying to dig up some wildflowers to transplant around the garden, but Mom explained that they wouldn't take.

"You can't grow them, Annie," she said. "Wildflowers have to grow by themselves."

After Mom was gone, the garden went neglected but we still called the space "Mom's garden." And now wildflowers have started growing there.

I told Dad that I was going to weed everything out except the wildflowers, and start over. Mom would like that. I told Dad that I needed his help to do it. We could get some iced tea and work together getting grass stains on our knees, and later sit on the wraparound porch with our feet up like Mom did. I'd wear his Red Sox hat, like Mom did. Always with the brim forward, the way Mom said to wear it. Maybe I'd even have a cigarette—a Marlboro light, like her. Just one.

Dad nodded. "We'll do that for sure, sweetheart. Your mom would love it. Except for the cigarette. She wouldn't want you to smoke."

"Is everything going to be okay tomorrow?"

"We'll see."

"Do you think Mr. Aireys is doing a good job?"

"I guess he's probably doing the best he can."

"Dad, was I a good kid?"

Dad turned on his side and looked at me. "You still are."

"I mean, you wanted me to try out for track and soccer but I wouldn't, even though I knew how great I'd look in those shorts."

Dad laughed and leaned over and kissed me.

"It was just because none of my friends were trying out."

"I know."

"But I never got electric hair or tattoos, Dad."

"Yes, that was nice of you."

"And I never went Goth."

"Oh, thank you very much."

"I think I was afraid that Mom would come back and be disappointed. Do you remember when I left for school in that monster sweater and a padded bra? I didn't know it was a contradiction."

"I know, sweetie." Dad put his arm around me.

"I think that if Mom had been around I probably would have resisted her and fought her too."

"It's pretty normal, kiddo."

"You know what I envied the soccer girls the most? How sometimes when they'd score a goal they'd tear off their jerseys to show their sports bras, and then fall to their knees like the girls in the Olympics."

"You would have been the hottest, Annie."

"Do you think I look like Mom?"

"You know you do. Except for the navel piercing."

"That was just a thing."

"I know. I hope I wasn't an awful father. We needed your mom every day."

"I learned something from you, Dad. Teach my children and then wait for them."

He smiled. "We live life forwards, Annie. But we understand it backwards."

"Were you a good kid? Grandpa Sam never said."

"I was perfect. Never cried, never stole anything, always got gold stars and all A's. I did exactly what your grandparents said."

"Yeah, right. That means you were a real monster."

"I was a kid, Annie. I was just a kid, that's all."

29

**How bold one gets when
one is sure of being loved.
-Sigmund Freud**

DAD IS SWORN IN.

"Simon, it's a big day."

"It sure is. Finally."

"Why do you want to testify, Simon?"

"I want the truth to come out. I want everyone to hear it from me."

"So you have nothing to hide?"

"Nothing at all." Dad looked at the jurors and then at me. He smiled his great smile.

"Good. Can you tell the jury how long you were married to your wife, Sunny."

"A little over ten years. I'm still married to her."

"Was it a happy marriage."

"I can't imagine a happier one. She was terrific, and I was so fortunate to have her."

"No arguments? No quarrels?"

"Not very often, even over the little stuff like who changed the diapers last or which movie to watch. We always looked out for each other."

"So, nothing big?"

"I don't remember even one argument that was remotely big."

"And you have two children?"

"Annie and Veronica. Annie's over there." He pointed. "She's nineteen now, and Veronica is thirteen."

"Thank you, Simon. Can you tell the jury, in your own words, what happened the morning your wife Sunny went missing?"

"Yes. There wasn't anything really unusual about that morning, except that the girls slept a little later for some reason, so Sunny and I stayed in bed a little longer. We were up by seven-thirty, and had to get ready for my mother and father who were driving up from the City to spend some time with the girls. They were planning on getting to our place around noon. Sunny liked to have the house looking nice for them and have the girls already dressed. She wanted everything ready when they arrived."

"What else?"

"Sunny realized we needed some things from the store and asked me if I could go get them. That was about 9:45, no later."

"But you didn't have to go to the store right then, did you?"

"I knew the day was special for Sunny because she knew how precious extended family is. Since the girls' grandparents were going to be there, she asked me to go to the store; I went pretty much right away. We were like that, trying to anticipate how we could help each other."

"And you came back when?"

"Maybe forty-five minutes later. Sunny only asked for a few things. Mitch's Market had everything we needed."

"What happened when you returned home?"

"First, I noticed the front door was locked. It was almost never locked because it's so safe in Windham. People hardly ever lock their doors even at night. I had to get out my keys to let myself in."

"What did you find?"

"The stereo was still playing. I could hear Annie upstairs and Veronica was playing downstairs. I didn't see Sunny. But her car was there. I called for her, and then I looked for her, but she wasn't anywhere. The girls didn't know where she was either. I went to the neighbors' next, and then I called the police. I didn't wait. The locked door was strange. I sensed something was maybe. . . maybe really wrong. Almost right away Trooper Wood and some other officers came. Later my parents came."

"Did you participate in the search for Sunny?"

"I did. I searched with them for nearly two days. I contacted the TV stations too, and the radio, but I guess it wasn't a story for them."

"Why not?"

"They said husbands and wives leave each other all the time. But they didn't know Sunny. And they didn't know me."

"How long did you continue to search for Sunny?"

"From the day she was gone until they found her. She was always on my mind. After it was in the papers for a day or so, it was forgotten. But I put up fliers everywhere. I looked for her every time I went anywhere or picked up newspapers hoping she'd be mentioned in it. I watched the news for any missing person who had just been found. I needed to find her no matter what had happened to her."

"And did you have anything to do with what did happen to her, Simon?"

"No, nothing at all."

"Thank you, Simon. Now there are some other questions, or rather, uncertainties, about some other things that I need to ask you about. "

"I know."

"Some of this may be difficult or awkward, but of course it's best that everything come out."

"You want to know about the handcuffs."

"Yes, that's right. We want to know about the handcuffs. Did you buy them?"

"I did."

"Were they sent to your office?"

"Yes."

"Did your secretary see them, just as she described?"

"Yes, exactly as Anita described."

"Were they in a blue box, and were there three of them?"

"Yes, three."

"Did Sunny know that you had bought them?"

Dad was silent. He looked over at me for what seemed like a long time. Mr. Aireys tried to smile to cover up Dad's hesitation. After a long moment he tried again.

"Simon, did Sunny know that you had bought them?"

Dad continued to look at me.

"Simon, please. Did you show them to Sunny?"

More silence.

"Simon?"

"I'm sorry, but I'm invoking spousal privilege."

30

**Against all the evidence of his senses, a man
who is in love declares that "I" and "you" are one.
And he is prepared to behave as if it were a fact.
-Sigmund Freud.**

MR. AIREYS WAS STUNNED. I remember him stepping back then touching his hand to his forehead and looking at my dad with an uncomfortable smile. This wasn't part of the plan. It wasn't going to win anyone over. It was, in fact, a disaster. Mr. Aireys moved his head left and right as if looking for answers in the air. He turned to the judge.

"Your Honor, I'd like a recess so I can speak to my client."

"Fifteen minutes, then, Mr. Aireys."

"No recess." It was my dad speaking.

"We have to talk, Simon. Thank you, Your Honor."

"Your Honor, I'll be dismissing my attorney if he won't continue to represent me in the way I see fit."

I was proud of Dad. I was beaming at him when he looked over at me.

Mr. Aireys walked in a small circle. He looked up at the judge, smiled and said he'd continue. He was determined to salvage

Dad's testimony. The best thing he could do now was to try to undercut what Ms. Davies would be asking.

"Simon, do you understand the New York State laws regarding spousal privilege?"

"Yes. Courts cannot force husbands and wives to disclose the contents of confidential communications made during marriage, or even after they are divorced. That's New York Code 4502(b)."

"Are you're aware that spousal privilege applies only when both spouses are alive."

"Yes. I also know that the reason for the handcuffs is nobody's business but Sunny's and mine. Things are private between a husband and wife, confidential. They aren't anybody's business."

Mr. Aireys took a huge breath and looked at his assistants. He was panicking. He had to persuade Dad to change his mind.

"But do you see how it will look, having these handcuffs in your possession and not explaining it to the jury?"

"It might look like I'm respecting my wife's memory. I don't want anyone to think badly of Sunny. It's her case too. As far as I'm concerned our relationship is confidential."

"Now Simon," he pleaded, "you came here to answer questions freely, and now you aren't. You're refusing to . . ." Mr. Aireys couldn't find the words. "Ms. Davies is waiting for the opportunity to prove that you lack credibility."

"I know. "

"You're not protecting Sunny from anything criminal, Simon. Ms. Davies will say that Sunny isn't the one on trial for anything. There's nothing that would implicate her in any wrongdoing. So there's no spousal privilege."

"Even so, you're asking about something private between Sunny and me. Husband and wife."

"Simon, the jury may not understand!"

"Yes, they will. Spousal exclusion is to protect the sanctity of the marital bond."

"Ms. Davies will say that there isn't any bond because you and Sunny aren't married."

"If she says there's no bond, then she doesn't know Sunny and me. I don't care what she says. I control the privilege because Sunny can't. Sunny hasn't committed any crime. I haven't either."

"Then why are you here if not to testify fully?"

"I asked to take the stand to present myself to the jury. To let them see me. So I could talk about my love for Sunny. Not to reveal anything that's none of anyone's business. I think they'll understand that what went on is between Sunny and me. I hope they will."

Mr. Aireys took another deep breath.

"Your Honor, I have no further questions."

31

One is very crazy when in love.
-Sigmund Freud

Ms. Davies stood at the side of the witness stand and directed her speech to my dad.

"Mr. Taylor, I want to thank you for coming today to testify."

"It's Dr. Taylor."

"Yes, I'm sorry. Dr. Taylor, thank you for coming to testify. You didn't have to. You could have remained silent throughout the whole trial. I'm not going to ask you about how you and Sunny used the handcuffs. Because, of course, what you did is between you two. I respect that. Now, Dr. Taylor, in your reading of the New York State law, do you understand that there is *no* spousal privilege if one spouse is accused of committing a crime against the other spouse?"

"Yes, but that's only if one spouse is accused *by the other spouse*. Sunny isn't accusing me of anything."

"Sunny isn't here to accuse you."

"And she wouldn't."

"Isn't it true that spousal privilege is obtained only when the couple is still married . . .?

"We *are* still married."

"Don't interrupt me, sir. Spousal privilege is obtained when the couple is married, and even after divorce neither can speak about the other; but if one of the parties dies, spousal privilege ends. Isn't that right?"

"That's correct. Sunny isn't here to protect the right, so I have to do it for her."

"Where in the law does it say that one person is permitted to protect another person's rights, Dr. Taylor?"

"I don't care. Sunny's not here to assert her privilege, so I have to. "

"I don't think you understand the law, Dr. Taylor."

"The courts have ruled that marital privilege is to protect and strengthen the marital relationship, and any communication is confidential 'if it is prompted by the affection, confidence and loyalty engendered by such relationship.' *People v. Mills* and *Poppe v Poppe*."

"Let's move on then. You said that you were never angry with Sunny, that you never fought."

"That's right."

"She was arrested twice, isn't that so?"

"Yes."

"Both times she was arrested for assault with intention to do bodily harm."

"Sunny wouldn't hurt anyone. And she didn't."

"But when she was arrested, weren't you angry?"

"More upset than angry, I'd say."

"You weren't angry? Not at all?"

"Maybe some. "

"But you had forgotten about that anger when you testified just now, right?"

"Objection, Your Honor. Badgering the witness."

"Objection sustained. Move on, Ms. Davies."

"What else have you conveniently forgotten, Dr. Taylor?"

"Objection!"

"Sit down, Mr. Aireys! Move on, Ms. Davies."

"Please tell the Court this, Dr. Taylor. When Ms. Anita Rogers, your former secretary, testified that she saw the handcuffs on your desk at the office next to a blue box, was she correct?"

"As I've already said, the way Anita described our exchange is exactly the way I remember it."

"What were the handcuffs in your office for?"

Dad was silent.

"No need to answer, Dr. Taylor. Everyone knows what handcuffs are for."

"Objection!"

"Sustained. Ms. Davies, are you testifying about what they are for?"

"No, Your Honor. I was thinking out loud, is all. I apologize. Dr. Taylor, what are handcuffs usually used for?"

"The police use them for restraints."

"You admit that you bought those?"

"I do."

"Are you a police officer, Dr. Taylor?"

"No."

"And you bought three pairs in all, is that correct?"

"I did."

"Why three pairs? Why not one?"

"That's the way they came, as a set."

"They came in the blue box that Ms. Rogers saw in your office."

"I've already said that."

"When you took them home, were there two or three pairs in the box?"

"Objection. The witness never said he took them home." Mr. Aireys was just trying to disrupt Ms. Davies' questions.

"Sustained."

"Did you take them home, Dr. Taylor?"

"I did."

"When you took them home, did you take one, two, or three pairs home?"

"I took all three pairs home."

"That was some months before Sunny went missing. Is that correct?"

"Yes."

"When you opened the box, were all three pairs in it?"

"Objection. Dr. Taylor never said he opened the box."

"Did you open the box, Dr. Taylor?"

"When?"

"Any time after you got home with the blue box."

"Yes, I did."

"How many times?"

Dad doesn't answer.

"Your Honor, the witness won't answer this simple question."

"Dr. Taylor, you are directed to answer, please."

"I'm sorry, I don't remember how many times."

"Generally, tell the Court the number of times, Dr. Taylor. More than once? More than ten times?"

"I'm not going to answer that."

"Twice a day, Dr. Taylor?"

"Objection! He's already answered, and now she's badgering, Your Honor."

"I was just referring to Dr. Taylor's famous book. I'm sorry, Your Honor."

"Objection sustained. The witness already said he doesn't remember. The jury will have to decide whether he's credible or not. "

"Where did you keep the blue box?"

Silence.

"Did you keep it in the bedroom?"

"Yes. Later I moved it to Sunny's meditation room. "

"Did you notice that a pair was missing?"

"No."

"Thank you. Now Dr. Taylor, here's a copy of your book. Would you read the title for the Court?"

"Yes. *Twice a Day (Thank you)*."

"You didn't read: 'A Guide for Couples.' That is part of the title, is it not?"

"That's right."

"Would you read what you wrote on page ninety-one?"

Dad took the book. "It says . . ."

"Not '*It* says,' Dr. Taylor. Read what *you* say."

"What I say there doesn't refer to Sunny and me."

"Just read what you wrote, please. Not everyone here has had the benefit of your great wisdom."

"Objection!"

"Sustained. Keep it going, Ms. Davies."

"Just read, please, Dr. Taylor."

"'Everyone has fantasies and urges that may result in behaviors that could be misconstrued as an attempt to harm someone. These behaviors might seem offensive to others, even perverted, because of our many taboos. I call this societal offense 'the tyranny of our social shoulds.'"

"Go on."

"'We must fearlessly confront our deepest urges. They are irrational—by which I mean they are not governed by reason—because they are so deep inside of us. Living our deepest urges fully is much preferred to years of psychoanalysis, trying to dismiss the urges, or trying to think them away. To live them out is important for human growth.'"

"Do you still believe what you wrote, Dr. Taylor?"

"You'll find much the same idea in any D.H. Lawrence novel."

"But do you still believe what you wrote, Dr. Taylor?"

"I do."

"Are you a sadist, Dr. Taylor?"

"No."

"Was Sunny a masochist? Did she enjoy pain?"

"No, no, no. Not at all! Not at all!"

"Did she enjoy being restrained, Dr. Taylor."

"Objection. That would be relevant to what?"

"Sustained. Keep going Ms. Davies."

"Did *you* enjoy being restrained, Dr. Taylor."

"Same objection."

"Sustained again. I said to keep it going, Ms. Davies."

"I'm trying, Your Honor. "Dr. Taylor, are you familiar with the phrase, 'Inside every person is another person deprived of what he wants'?"

"Yes, of course. I've said that to my patients. "

"Were you talking about yourself?"

"Yes, of course."

"What does it mean, that 'inside every person is another person deprived of what he wants'?"

"It means that there are urges in each of us that we don't understand."

"Does that include you too?"

"Of course. And you too, Ms. Davies. "

"Please don't analyze me, Dr. Taylor."

"I'm just saying that I'm referring to all of us."

"Oh, so even inside each of the jury members, then. They have urges they don't understand?"

"I believe so. "

"Thank you, sir. Now how would you describe this other person inside you?"

"I don't see how that's germane. "

"Oh, it is. Are you a multiple personality type?"

"No."

"Do you have a personality that we don't know about in this courtroom?"

"No."

"Do you have urges?"

"Yes."

"Urges you can't control?"

"No, of course not. "

"Are you a psychopath?"

"Objection, Your Honor. "

"I'll allow it. He's the doctor. "

"No. Not at all."

"But there is another person inside you with urges?"

"Of course."

"Another sexual person?"

"Of course."

"Something hidden inside of you?"

"We all have that."

"Something you don't understand?"

"Yes, as does everyone."

"A destructive part? Do we all have that?"

"I don't know if everyone does, but . . ."

"Dr. Taylor, do you have a phobia?"

"Objection! Relevance."

"I'll allow it."

"Dr. Taylor, do you have your own phobia?"

"Everyone is afraid of something, Ms. Davies."

"And you? What are you afraid of?"

"Objection again. Relevance, Your Honor."

"Objection sustained. Ms. Davies you haven't established the reason for your line of questioning."

"If I could have a little leeway, Your Honor."

"Go on, then."

"What is the term for a mirror phobia, Dr. Taylor?"

"It's called catoptrophobia."

"Do you suffer from that?"

"No."

"Are you sure?"

"Objection. Asked and answered, Your Honor."

"Of course I'm sure."

"I have a mirror in my bag here, Dr. Taylor."

"Objection!"

"It's right here, Your Honor."

"Sustained. Move on. "

"Let me get it out."

"That's enough Ms. Davies!"

She quickly pulled out a compact mirror.

"Your Honor!" Mr. Aireys shouted.

"Ms. Davies, put the mirror away and continue with your questions."

She held it up, challenging Dad. He flinched just a little, and then looked directly into the mirror. He stiffened and I saw him raise his hand to his side. Then he put it in his lap and continued to look into the mirror.

"Ms. Davies, you're almost in contempt."

She put the mirror away.

"Do you ever panic, Dr. Taylor?"

"Objection!"

"Sustained. Move it along! Move it along!"

"Dr. Taylor, you are a Freudian, are you not?"

"I've relied on Freud's insights to help my patients."

"Freud thought that women are childlike dolls, didn't he? He considered women to be ministering angels for men's pleasure, didn't he?"

"Objection. One question at a time. The witness can't possibly know what Freud thought."

"Sustained. I'm getting really impatient, Ms. Davies."

"No, I'll answer that. Dr. Freud never said anything remotely like that, and unlike you, Ms. Davies, I've never tried to analyze him. Sunny wasn't a childlike doll. She was a whole and wonderful woman, as complex as any of us. Even you, Ms. Davies."

"Your Honor. Now the witness is analyzing me!"

"Sustained, I guess. If that's an objection."

"Are you a stable person, Dr. Taylor?"

"Yes, I am."

"Did you kill Sunny?"

"I did not."

"Did you take her from your house?"

"I did not."

"Did you take her to the woods?"

"I did not."

"Was she already dead when you took her there, Dr. Taylor?"

Silence.

"Did you leave her there in the woods?"

"I did not."

"Leave her to die?"

Silence.

"No other questions for the learned witness, Your Honor."

"Dr. Taylor, you may return to your seat."

32

**A man should not try to eliminate his complexes.
He should try to get in accord with them— they are
legitimately what direct his conduct in the world.
-Sigmund Freud**

THE JUDGE HADN'T LET TV CAMERAS IN THE COURT, so the best the journalists could do was quote or paraphrase what Dad had said. Or report what they *thought* they heard. Will Halverton had his own column that was reprinted in many places online. He wrote that Dad was evasive and obstinate. He portrayed Dad as a deviant freak. Not in so many words, but that's what a reader had to come away with. The *Times* kept its coverage below the fold, the local papers above the fold, and the *Post* ran a one-inch-thick headline because it was a slow day. They included mention of Kathy Booth as well, who still claims she had an affair with Dad, and that he had held her down and all. The word "adulterer" wasn't used though it was implied. Dad came off in all the accounts as a debased psychiatrist who wrote about sex and was fixated on sadism and masochism.

The day after Dad testified, the jury was given instructions. They left the courtroom for deliberations. Dad and I didn't say anything about the trial on the way home or at all that evening, but Dad did tell me that we needed to talk about something, and that I should let him know when it was a good time for me. I thought he wanted to discuss what happened if we lost the case, but that wasn't it.

I didn't set a time for our talk. It just sort of happened. I had grabbed something to drink from the fridge and plunked myself down at the kitchen table next to Dad. He was reading some legal papers. He set them aside. He smiled, as though he was especially proud of me. I knew the moment for our talk had come.

He started by saying he was going to talk like a shrink for a moment, if I didn't mind.

"Sure," I said.

"There are basically two kinds of marriages, sweetheart," he started. "In one kind, the couple knows what they are doing, and in the other kind, they don't."

I nodded.

"In other words," he went on, "there are two types of marriages — *conscious* and *unconscious*."

Dad paused as if searching for words. I nodded again to encourage him.

"The *unconscious* marriage," he said, "is when you live together and you relate to each other in a knee-jerk way. With your first impulse, usually a reaction from out of your past. That's what most people have. But your mom and I, well, she had her religion and her meditation, and it actually put her ahead of me, even with all my studies, and especially in handling a conscious relationship because she was so attentive to everything around her. Much more than I was."

"You mean she didn't automatically react when something went wrong."

"Yes, it's big part of a conscious marriage," he continued. "A *conscious* marriage is also when each partner helps the other to uncover what's buried inside them. Not just suddenly reacting, spewing some words or doing something impulsively, but living consciously, thoughtfully. Your Mom and I didn't talk about our needs much because it wasn't necessary. It's like when you're walking down the street with someone you really like and you sort of just fall in step with each other. That was our relationship, Annie, your mom's and mine. Neither of us had to lead. We just fell in step with each other."

I knew where Dad was going with this and how hard it was for him. He was trying to explain the handcuffs without really explaining them.

"You know about my . . . my challenge," he said. "The mirrors. I wasn't truthful about it on the stand."

"You lied."

"I know. I just can't discuss it in public. I guess that's a real weakness in me, and my shame." I started to say something, but he held up his hand. "I haven't been able to excavate why I have a mirror phobia, so it's like a fly or mosquito that won't go away. But you see how I deal with it, consciously breaking the thought loop."

I nodded again.

"Please understand that there will always be things that we won't understand about ourselves, and which will continue to affect us. My mirror issue is mostly only a problem when it affects me in public. Otherwise, who cares much? Certainly not your mom."

"Me either," I told him.

"I know. Your mom called it my little hiccup because it was such a tiny thing compared to everything else we had going that was so good and expansive and important.

"What I'm trying to say, Annie, is that there are always little things, oddities that make us who we are. Public things and private things too. Who knows where they come from? They could just be *us*, and nothing more. Nobody has it all figured out. That goes for romance too."

He paused and looked down, then looked back at me and continued. "Annie, when people are together a lot, privately and romantically I mean, and of course consciously, they catch on about the other, like two people falling in step. It seems easy. And natural. The most natural thing in the world."

"I think I understand, Dad," I said. I wanted to give him an out if he wanted one.

"Just listen a minute." He thought a few seconds more and then said, "Sometimes in private, we need the opposite of what we need in public. It's like a way to balance. Nobody is vivacious and bouncy all the time. There can be another part that's just as vital, though maybe very different. Your mom was so zippy and exuberant that she could wear people out. But she had other needs too."

He paused for what seemed like a long time.

"There was nothing else, Annie, besides the . . ." He couldn't say the word *handcuffs*. "None of that other stuff that people imagined." He looked at me to see if I believed him. I nodded that I did.

"We had a conscious marriage, not an unconscious one," he added after a time, and he looked real sad again. "Maybe that's all I want to say, Annie. Except that I really miss her."

Even though someone might trust someone as much as I trusted Dad, and even though that someone might keep saying she believes him, there is always that corner of doubt in her mind, a hidden presence when that person is accused of doing something awful. Since I'm trying to be as truthful as is humanly possible, I'll say now that I had tiny doubts all along, somewhere in a back corner of my mental closet. I admit it. But all those doubts vanished after Dad finished speaking.

Dad had to hold me because I was crying.

33

**Much of our highly valued culture
has been acquired at the cost of sexuality.
-Sigmund Freud**

EVERYONE SAYS THAT YOU NEVER KNOW WHAT A JURY WILL DO, and that you never know how much the press and the news shows have already affected them. They aren't supposed to read or watch anything, but they always do.

Mr. Aireys said what's done is done, and that he hoped that Dad's testimony could turn out to be the right thing after all. But I knew that while there weren't a lot of real facts against my dad, things still might not add up right in the jury members' minds. Mainly the missing pair of handcuffs that were on Mom. Dad had even admitted that he had ordered them. That he had them at home. The jury members knew that he and Mom had used them.

I hoped the jurors could still have some reasonable doubts.

I've seen live trials on TV and know that when the jury stays out a long time it's usually because the person is guilty. If you're going to send someone to prison forever then you have to be sure. You have to be certain that no one on the jury has doubts. Their decision doesn't just affect one person. It affects a whole family.

The jury was out from Wednesday until well into the next week. There were still columns in the papers about the case each day and a lot of coverage on the news, mainly speculating that the jury is thinking this or that. The reporters couldn't let the public forget about the case or they'd have to find a brand new story, and this one was too good to let go. They showed pictures of Christy Jones' parents again, as if that had anything to do with anything. And recounted what the woman had said about when she slept with Dad.

Thursday afternoon. We got the call. Dad dressed hurriedly, wearing his newest suit and a tie I had picked out for him. I checked it after he put it on. I checked his face too for any spots he had missed while shaving. There weren't any. The sun was out as I drove us in. Dad didn't put the top down or turn on the radio. I could have used a little of The Rascals', "A Beautiful Morning."

We drove mostly in silence, and when we got to the court-room we went to our seats. Grandpa Sam was there too, next to me in the first row. He was so solemn and tense. Grandma Janet hadn't come. I could hardly blame her. Christy Jones' parents were sitting in their usual places toward the front on the other side. Will Halverston was in his seat. I wanted to go over and slug him in the face.

Then the jury came in. I'd heard from TV shows that when the jury comes back you can often tell what their decision is by who they look at—the defendant or the district attorney. They filed to their places, looking only at the district attorney. I didn't see any-one look at Dad.

I didn't plan it, but I suddenly shot up and shouted—"*Look over here, will you! Look over here!*"

Now they did look. The whole courtroom looked, but only at me. Not at Dad. Then the jury members glanced away. In the silence that followed, the judge said nothing at all. He was his usual solemn-faced self. I sat down with my head in my hands.

Then the judge told Dad to rise. Dad glanced over at me first. He was checking to see if I was okay. I wasn't. I wanted to be home with Grandma Janet right then.

Dad got up.

I got up too, right behind him. I felt light-headed and the room was suddenly so hot.

The judge looked at me for a long moment, then reached out his hand and pointed for me to sit down. I wouldn't.

"Sit down, Miss!" he demanded.

I stood with my hands balled at my side. The bailiff started to move in my direction. But I was going to stand with Dad. No one was going to stop me.

Finally the judge turned to the jury.

Then the foreman read the verdict.

Then they put the handcuffs on my dad.

Then there were shouts and loud cheers. Even the judge couldn't control them.

34

**One day, in retrospect, the years of struggle
will strike you as the most beautiful.
-Sigmund Freud**

IF IT HADN'T BEEN FOR RAINBOW limping around nothing would have moved in our house. Grandpa Sam sat slumped in Dad's chair, stunned and grave. Veronica was face down and motionless on the couch. At first even Grandma Janet, the Saint-in-Waiting, was quiet too, but then she changed back into her usual messianic self, chipper and chirping about how God will intervene and everything will be okay. I wanted to look for a baseball bat. She quieted down when she saw Grandpa Sam's glare.

I went outside and sat on the swing, not moving, like a statue. No neighbors came by to see if we were okay or to ask if we needed anything. Not a single car drove down our street. I looked over at Mom's garden. I had planned to start planting, making it into a thing of beauty like Mom would have, but now I wouldn't be able to. The house was up for sale.

I thought about how there are two views of why people do bad things. One view is that we are naturally good and nice to each other, but civilization has stolen our goodness, so now we are greedy and aggressive and we hurt each other to get what we want. The other view is Freud's: He says that it's not society that makes us greedy and aggressive. That we are all naturally that way. We've always hurt each other, he says. Civilization exists to suppress that drive in us.

Sitting on the swing I knew which was true. Freud was wrong. There is nothing naturally greedy or aggressive about my dad. I wanted him back, and I would do anything to get him back.

A call came for me and I went inside to take it. It was Connie from school, my Asian friend with the blindfold. She was crying hysterically; she'd heard. I told her everything was going to be okay. But forty to life is not okay. I wasn't up for being Connie's therapist. I had to hang up on her.

Through the window I saw a van with a disc on top rolling up on the street. Almost immediately a second one appeared. The van doors slid open. Three people got out and started setting up equipment. Rainbow barked. Grandpa Sam stepped out onto the porch and stood there with his arm on the post, holding Rainbow by the collar, facing the people from the van with a frown and a scowl. He's an imposing figure, even at his age. A woman and cameraman stepped onto our walk, camera rolling as the reporter held her microphone out and started up toward the house. When they saw Grandpa Sam coming toward them with Rainbow they hurriedly packed up and left. No one was going to ask us *what it's like*. No one was going to ask us *how it feels*.

I had never felt rage such before, not like this. I wanted to scream. I wanted to throw things, everything. I know that not all dads are even close to being as great as my dad. Some drink too much and are vulgar and play around, or run off for a time, or forever. Simon Taylor hardly ever drank. He was refined and never played around. He would never run off, even for an hour. He took his responsibilities to heart and showed us how to be responsible. He showed us what a great dad and husband look like. No one can take that away.

I haven't mentioned where my mom is buried. After she was found, Dad was so much in shock that he wasn't sure if she should be buried here or back in Punjab. He wanted her here, but Mom's parents called every day, pleading for their lovely daughter to come home. Finally I took over the decision-making and announced that Mom would be buried here. There is an old graveyard between Windham and Ashland, and that's where she is.

Just before dark I got some flashlights, and Veronica and I went out to visit her.

35

**From error to error,
one finally discovers the truth.
-Sigmund Freud**

I STARTED MY LITTLE BOOK or whatever this is by remembering what Mom said — that truth is the only thing that mattered, and that I should pursue it at any cost. "Never be afraid of it," she always said to me. And now that I know the truth it's like a knife forever opening my veins.

I think that the deepest tragedies unfold slowly. There is always some kind of violence too. Afterward, sometimes long afterward, there is a grief that seems to linger everywhere. That's what happened here. And more.

It was a month after the trial. Veronica and I were still living at the house because it hadn't been sold yet; I was taking care of her, making the meals, checking her homework, generally trying to keep her spirits up, and mine too.

I was really doing nothing, just preparing sandwiches and milk. Usually my best thoughts come when I'm walking alone, or in the shower, or as I'm falling asleep. I'm not the only one, because that's when the conscious mind let's go for a while, and we permit the unconscious pieces to come together; a math problem solved or some conflict worked out inside us; a recognition, a sudden comprehension from deep down.

I was fixing sandwiches for Veronica and myself. I guess I had given up on everything and was resigned to my dad not ever being with us again. I spread mayo across the white bread, then two slices of tomato, a little lettuce, and some honey mustard because Veronica likes it so much. I got out some thin slices of ham and pressed them down on top. "No cheese," I called over to Veronica, "We need to get some cheddar. We're out."

"Just put some Parmesan on," she called back. "We've got that. Or something. Surprise me."

Surprise me.

I stopped. My hands went to the countertop to steady myself, my eyes staring into the cabinet at nothing.

Parmesan, and *surprise me.* There was a connection. I knew there was, the three words, like a kind of hidden logic. A straight line — A to B. *Parmesan — Surprise me.* But something was still missing.

Then it was coming, as if some unknown and sudden pressure was building and trying to pry itself out from my gut or my head, struggling to the surface. My heart pounded. I closed my eyes to clear away what I could, to be still, and to focus, so maybe I could will it through the distractions, whatever it was.

My mom was gone. My dad was gone.

Parmesan — Surprise me.

No, not a straight line, but a triangle was trying to form in my head: A to B to C. A corner was still missing. What was it?

Parmesan, and *surprise me.*

And what?

I knew the final piece was somewhere there, I could feel it. Maybe this was Freud's "subdued analysis" that he said was followed by a dream, an intuition, or an insight that finally pushes its way past the minutia that fills our day. All I know is that a clamoring voice was rising to the surface, a voice that had been there all along, now howling and stern.

Parmesan – Surprise me.

My dad going out to the store. My grandparents coming up. Grandma Janet going door-to-door in Hudson. My mom being gone.

Parmesan – Surprise me.

And something else. What?

The answer was there, somewhere, like the hovering stars are there, waiting through the daylight for their time, just as my dad had said.

And then the missing piece – a single word. I already had A to B.

Now I had C!

Yes, it had been there all along.

I finally knew. I *finally knew.*

I had gone through all the police reports a dozen times and had read all the papers and watched the investigative shows. But the answer wasn't there. It wasn't a neighbor who had taken Mom away. Or some pervert happening to drive by who lured her to his car, maybe asking for directions; or a stalker who had seen her in town or somewhere and had been following her, watching and waiting, and then taking advantage. There was only one explanation. I was gulping air now and had to slow my breathing down – breathe in, breath out. I *knew* who it was. I *knew* who it had to be.

I pushed the sandwiches away and grabbed Veronica. To Grandmother's house we would go.

36

**Whoever loves becomes humble. And those
who love have given up a part of their narcissism.
-Sigmund Freud**

"BUT WHERE ARE WE GOING?" Veronica asked when we got in the car. "I thought we were going to eat."

"Just put your seatbelt on," I told her. I saw Rainbow stumbling up from the creek toward us on his three legs. He was really old now, but moving as fast as he could. I got out and slid the seat forward for him and lifted him into the back with both hands.

"But where?" Veronica said.

"We're going to Grandma's."

She groaned, I'm sure anticipating being dragged off to some church somewhere, or having a mini catechism in her living room.

I went east, then south on the freeway, travelling faster than I ever had. I was like Mom, speeding along, passing everyone on the left and right. I didn't even watch the mirror for blue lights. I didn't care.

It usually took us two and half hours to get to Coopers Drive, in Saddle Rock, but I made it in two. My grandparent's home is a bungalow-type with red shingle siding and an attached garage. I parked in the driveway next to Grandma's station wagon, and let Rainbow out of the back. Veronica and I went up the walk past the daffodils and crocuses with Rainbow hobbling behind.

Grandma Janet had seen us from the window. She came to the door in a fluffy apron, wiping off her hands, her smile saying she was glad to see us.

"Oh, this is such a nice surprise," she said to us. "And Rainbow too. How nice."

She saw the look on my face. Furious. Determined. She just stood there blocking the doorway, not moving aside to invite us in. She knew. She knew that I knew. Yet still that same smile, the one that says that God and the saints are going to save us all from hell if we just have enough faith.

Veronica was already rolling her eyeballs, but stopped when I gave her my look.

I pushed past Grandma Janet and into the living room. She followed and tried to give me a hug me. I was rigid.

"Tea?" she said, nervously. "Yes, let's all have some tea." Grandma Janet headed off directly to the kitchen. "What a nice surprise," she said again, over her shoulder.

It was iced tea, and Veronica and I sat on couch, Grandma Janet in a chair facing us, still holding that smile in place.

"I *know*, Grandma." I said.

She looked at me, her smile starting to droop.

"I *know*," I said again, more sternly this time, my hands making a fist.

She forced her smile back in place like everything was okay.

"*Parmesan*," I said. "And *surprise*." I took a breath and stared at her. "And *bicycles*."

Grandma Janet's eyes jerked away frantically, racing around the room like she was following something in the air. I waited for her to deny it. To say I was wrong. Or maybe demand that we leave. But instead her face crumpled like an old tissue paper, and her shoulders started shaking. She leaned back, spilling some ice tea but not even noticing it.

"I really tried, Annie," she said, and made an effort to look at me, but then quickly turned away. "I really tried," she repeated.

Veronica went over to her and put her hand on Grandma's shoulder. "What is it?" she asked, sympathetically. Veronica still didn't understand.

"I shouldn't have gone out that day, to Hudson," she said, her face in her hands now. She was sobbing. "We should have gone up together."

I got up, my hands in a fist at my side. "Veronica, can you leave us alone?"

"No, I'm here."

"Veronica."

"I'm staying." She reached around Grandma Janet and pulled her close, holding her.

"I prayed so hard for his soul," Grandma Janet went on, and then lapsed into silence.

I waited, trying to control myself, fighting every urge to just grab her and shake the words out.

She sat up stiffly. "He's a monster. I knew it. It wasn't the first time. I tried to protect him, to save him, but it's no use. I love my son so much."

"You *love* him!" I shouted.

She held that stiff posture, looking around the room as if for an escape.

"A monster," she said again, finally looking at us directly. "A *fucking* asshole. You don't know. I'm so sorry. I'm so sorry for you girls."

Veronica looked at me. We had never heard Grandma Janet swear before, not even a "heck" or a "damn." Veronica thought she was talking about our dad.

"I saw the marks on him. The next day. We stayed as long as we could at the house after . . . after Sunny was gone, but we had to leave—the business, the fucking bike store, and everything."

Veronica pulled her tighter. "What are you saying?"

"We got back home late and we went right to bed. The next morning I saw him coming out of the shower. There were marks on him, they were all over him, black and gray marks, and red swellings.

"Grandpa?" Veronica said.

"I knew then, Annie," she said, looking at me directly. "I knew it then, but I didn't know all of it for sure, or I tried not to know it, until much later after they found her. Then I knew." Grandma Janet stood up with her tea. She looked from me to Veronica, no smile, no happy tilt of the head, rigid as stone.

"He came up to bring the bikes, do you remember? He was going to meet me in Hudson and we'd bring them up together. But he came up earlier to be the one who gave them to you. He always wanted to be the one who gave you things. To surprise you." She turned to Veronica. "Don't you see?" Her eyes were pleading now. "Don't you see? *He's* the one who locked the door."

Veronica still didn't comprehend.

"Sunny always ran out to meet us and give us hugs. She was so wonderful, and I never told her that. I've tried to imagine it. No, I've tried not to imagine it. How it happened. That bully. He wanted to get his hands on her. He wanted to touch her, I knew it. There were complaints at the store from pretty girls coming in with their bikes. He'd ask them to sit on the bike so he could position the seat just right for them, but I knew what he was doing. Some of them knew too. I'd see how he hugged Sunny each time we came up, and again later when we left. It was too much, too close, hand a little low or something. Do you remember what she was wearing that day?"

I nodded as I visualized it. It was Dad's blue and green flannel shirt and those lose jeans with sneakers, her wonderful hair braided. Then, finally, only pieces of Mom and her clothing were left.

"I can imagine her," Grandma Janet went on. "So pretty, and I never told her that, I wish I had told her." She seemed to swallow as if getting her breath. "I don't know if he waited until your father was gone, or if it just happened like that, Simon not being there when he arrived with the bicycles. But I know she ran out, and they hugged. And then he touched her. I'm sure of it."

Still standing, Grandma moved her hand to her breast as she went on. "Sunny wouldn't understand, of course, she wouldn't. She'd be surprised, thinking at first that it was a mistake, and then shocked when she realized it wasn't. She'd step away. Then he'd grab her and say something—that he was sorry or something, that it was a mistake. But Sunny would know it wasn't. It was out of hand already. The bully. Then he'd grab her, and she would panic. Then he would panic and try to explain, try to persuade her. But you couldn't fool Sunny. She was like that, so good, so perfect that she couldn't be fooled. And she would fight him with everything."

Veronica backed away from Grandma and looked toward me.

"He had to hide it all, you see," Grandma went on. She reached in her apron pocket and pulled out a hanky. "He couldn't be found out. I didn't know why he had the handcuffs or where he got them, but I'd found them under the seat in our car even before she was missing. He must have found them one of the times he was babysitting, and had gone through your parent's things. I can't think of any other way. Then he gave me that fucking glare of his that said shut your face, then tried to tell me they were for our protection. I didn't know anything else then, until they found the other pairs. He had the missing pair." She was gasping now. "It's not my fault, you see," she said.

I came closer to Grandma Janet, and stood facing her now. "Not your *fault*," I said, my voice low and full of anger. "What *is* your fault is *knowing*, and doing *nothing*! *Nothing* for your son! *You did nothing!*"

Grandma Janet nodded. "Can you forgive me? At least you two? I prayed so hard after I saw the marks. They were so ugly. I prayed that I was all wrong. I went to church more, and tried to save people, but it was me. I was the terrible one."

She was sobbing again, leaning into her hands. "I was the terrible one," she repeated, "the one who couldn't stand up. Your mom was so gorgeous . . ." Grandma Janet's voice faded to nothing.

Now I was trembling, still with anger but also with joy, and trying to hold myself together.

"We can fix it," I said. "We can fix everything, Grandma. You can tell the police. The D.A. We'll have Dad back with us. He can come home."

"He just left her there. He didn't even cover her. *Fucking bastard.*"

But now we had the truth. The whole truth. They'd have to let Dad go. He'd be home by Sunday with me and Veronica and Rainbow. We'd be a family again. I started to cry with relief.

"At least it's over, Grandma. It's over. We can fix everything now."

37

The first request of civilization is justice.
-Sigmund Freud

I WENT TO THE PHONE AND GOT MR. AIREYS' NUMBER. I called him right away. Grandma Janet was still standing in the living room, her head hanging over Veronica's shoulder now, sobbing loudly.

Mr. Aireys seemed genuinely surprised, like even he'd thought my dad was guilty. He didn't believe me at first when I told him what Grandma Janet had just said, but when he started believing me, his voice changed. I remember thinking how pleased he sounded, like he'd won the case after all. That's all that mattered to him. He said he was going to call Ms. Davies. He hung up.

Ms. Davies called within fifteen minutes. She wanted to speak to Grandma Janet. "She can't right now," I told her. "She can't."

"I need to speak to her right away, in my office then. Three-thirty. I have time." She hung up.

I took the Saab and drove us right over to Ms. Davies' office. We waited outside in the hallway, and Ms. Davies finally came out and motioned for us to come inside. Grandma Janet looked like she was going to collapse, but then stiffened and walked into the office with us. She told Ms. Davies everything.

Ms. Davies was skeptical at first; a family trick, the killer's mother coming forth with a story. Finally she began to believe Grandma.

I walked over to Ms. Davies' desk where she was leaning forward, head in hands, thinking.

"We can start over," I said. "Right?"

Silence from Ms. Davies.

"Right?" I asked again.

"No."

"Put Grandma Janet on the stand this time."

She was shaking her head.

"What?"

"She can't testify."

"Why not?"

"There's nothing I can do," Ms. Davies said. "There's nothing I can do."

"WHAT THE FUCK TO YOU MEAN THERE'S NOTHING YOU CAN DO!"

She jerked back, startled, then composed herself. She looked away as she shook her head. "You don't understand, Annie," she said quietly. "I'm *so* sorry. There's nothing I can do. There's nothing anyone can do."

38

**Love and work
are the cornerstones of our humanness.
-Sigmund Freud**

MOM WAS GONE. Now Dad was gone too. And the house was up for sale. Grandma Janet was now living alone and taking care of Veronica while I was at school. She kicked Grandpa Sam out. He still runs his bicycle store. Sam the bully. Sam the murderer.

Grandma Janet is stronger now and wants to testify. Her Saint-in-Waiting complex has finally turned her into somewhat of a real saint. She really wants to tell the truth. But she can't. Grandpa Sam has to permit it. And he isn't about to. The legal codes. The law is the law. *Spousal privilege*. No exceptions. It's the same in every state. All their conversations and all that they know about each other are inadmissible in court. Even if they got divorced she wouldn't be allowed to testify. *Rules of evidence*. No breach is ever permitted. Ever. Only after Grandpa Sam dies can Grandma Janet come forward and tell the court what she knows. Only then can the court listen to her.

Sometimes the truth is delayed. Sometimes the truth just doesn't matter. People tell me it isn't personal. But it is. *It's always personal.*

I finally found out what's behind Dad's mirror phobia. Grandma Janet told me that when my dad was a boy, Grandpa Sam used to berate him over the smallest things. He would make him stand naked in front of a mirror and belittle him; his grades weren't just right, he dropped the ball in a Little League game, he was unhappy about something. Nothing he did was perfect. Grandpa would make him stand there and he would slap his head from behind and kick his ankles and make him stare into the mirror at himself: Simon the culprit, Simon the dawdler, Simon the failure.

Though the D.A.s office said they couldn't reverse Dad's sentence, I knew the media would write about it. So I called them immediately. They did run the story, but only once, and that was the end of it. Other news items were more important now. Other trials and other people missing, I suppose.

So that's that. The court system and the media will do nothing. But *I* will. I will do it. I know that Grandpa Sam tests bikes after he fixes them, rides them down Lafayette to Prince Street, changing gears, checking the brakes.

I know what will happen. I can see it in my mind. One day soon he will come to a bad end right there on Prince Street. My greatest pleasure will be that I'll happen to be in the City that day, driving by that corner. I'm a good driver, but not that good. Everybody makes mistakes. Hit and runs happen all the time. Even if the authorities find me, I don't care. My hair will be braided. I'll be wearing Mom's favorite barrette. I'll be driving Dad's car. After the accident, Grandma Janet will be able to testify.

Until that day, I am going to visit Dad every week. He's at Fallsburg, a place for "serious offenders." Until we spoke the other day he hadn't been communicating at all; he was probably still bewildered, depressed, or maybe wanting to spare us the pain of talking to a dad who's behind bars.

When we spoke, I told him that Rainbow is no longer with us. I found him down by the creek.

"I'm so sorry, baby," he said.

"He was worn out, Dad," I said. "Running on three legs all these years."

"I'm sorry, baby," he said again. "We'll all miss him."

After a moment he asked, "What about school?"

"Dad, what about Grandpa Sam? Have you tried to speak to him? Get him to admit it."

"I tried, but he's a stone wall. I can't even think about him now, Annie. It's too much. I'm more worried about you right now. And Veronica. Tell me how school is."

"It's going okay."

"How's math?"

"Okay."

"Just okay?"

"The usual. Maybe a little better than usual," I added with a laugh. "I'm reading *The Ego and the Id.*

"Heady stuff," Dad said with his own laugh, but then grew serious. "Remember what I said, about being careful . . ."

"Because things can stick to you. I remember."

"Good. Anything else?"

"Like what, Dad?"

"I guess, like boys."

"You mean men."

"Oh God, I hope not, baby."

"Dad."

"Well, tell me."

"There might be someone. Maybe."

"Might, maybe. So tell me about him. What's his name?"

"Dad. I haven't known him very long."

"He didn't tell you his name?"

"Dad!" I said with a laugh. "At the right moment, okay?"

He was quiet and I knew he was thinking about boys. "You don't have to say it, Dad. I already know."

Then Dad told me to take the house off the market. The bond had been paid back so the house was paid for. He wanted me to have it. He said he still had some money and that he'd get someone to take care of the grass and all so that I could go there when I'm not in school.

"You can sit on the porch and put your feet up and cross your ankles, just like your mom did," he said. "Bring your new friend, too. Only on the porch though. You can wear my Red Sox hat."

"But only with the brim toward the front, the way Mom liked it."

"That's right."

"Can I have a Marlboro Light, too? Like her. Just one?"

"Don't you smoke, Annie," he said, pretending to be stern. Then he laughed softly through the phone, as if remembering things, and I remembered how my dad used to be.

He added, "I'd really love it, Annie, if you did everything the way your mom did. She was so terrific. So strong."

"I'm not strong, Dad. I'm not." I started crying. "I wish I could be strong, like Mom."

"Baby."

"I'm okay, Dad," I said, still crying.

"Your mom was always trying to make things right."

"I know."

"That's all I want, Annie."

I gathered myself. "Okay," I told him. "That's what I'll do, Dad. I'll try to make everything right. Just like Mom did."

"That's so good, baby."

"I promise you that I will."

A note from Peter Gilboy

I hope you enjoyed Annie's Story.
And I hope you'll review it on Amazon,
Goodreads, Barnes & Noble,
or another place of your choice.
We independent authors depend on reviews.
And your review is very much appreciated.
Thank you.

Peter

Also, feel free to drop me a personal note:
Hello@PeterGilboy.com
www.PeterGilboy.com

If you're a writer, please see www.FictionWriterBlog.com

And don't forget
Madeleine's Kiss
by Peter Gilboy

"Uniquely Gripping"
"Defies the common label of thriller or mystery"

CPSIA information can be obtained at www.ICGtesting.com
Printed in the USA
BVOW01s2132070816

458229BV00004BA/169/P